And Not To Yield

A STORY OF THE OUTWARD BOUND SCHOOL OF ADVENTURE

AND NOT TO YIELD

A STORY OF THE OUTWARD BOUND SCHOOL OF ADVENTURE by ALAN VILLIERS

ILLUSTRATED BY JEAN MAIN AND DAVID COBB

CHARLES SCRIBNER'S SONS · NEW YORK

PRINTED IN THE UNITED STATES OF AMERICA

Foreword

THE real *Warspite* is a powerful big ketch of about 100 tons which sails in the Irish Sea from the port of Aberdovey, in North Wales. She races through Bardsey Sound, beats off the Causeway buoy and rounds the Bwch, and sails through the channel over the Dovey Bar many a time. Her crew is invariably a watch from the Outward Bound Sea School—twelve boys. I sailed the *Warspite* for her first season of this work, and the story is based upon that experience—*based* upon, I say, and not a factual account of it. We were never, by the grace of the Lord, blown out of St. Tudwal's Roads, though I was blown away from Nevin, and I had the mainsail thrash to pieces in an ugly squall off the South Stack, and the engine was terrible. That's been changed. There's a good new diesel in the *Warspite* now and, I'm afraid, little prospect that any watch will get the chance I've given my imaginary group in the story.

But I've had a watch just like this aboard many a time, and I don't doubt they'd have handled the ship quite well if there had really been an emergency.

And the *Warspite has* made that inner passage of the Causeway, though, I'm glad to say, not under conditions quite so desperate as I've used in the book.

ALAN VILLIERS

Contents

1

At Aberdovey

THE big black ketch came racing in the squall, the spume flying before her and over her and the cold wind roaring in her rigging. She was heeled over like a racing yacht, though she was carrying only reefed mains'l, a reefed mizzen, and a storm fore staysail. She was lofty, powerful, and fast, and she fairly tore through the water as the squall passed over her. The Outer Buoy leaped and jumped in the boiling sea and the whole Bar was a thunder of breakers, so that it was almost frightening to look at it.

The wind had been from the north earlier. Now it was from the west, blowing hard, and freshening in the squalls. There was still something of the northerly sea running in the bay, and now it converged with the sea racing in from the wild Atlantic to set up a violent turbulence upon the Bar, which was bad enough at any time. The big red recall flag was flying at the little wharf, for the boats to come back, the whalers and the cutters that had been at work in the estuary of the Dovey. The bad weather had come up quickly, as it so often did at any port where the North Atlantic was so close outside. The River Dovey flowed down from the hills of Wales into Cardigan Bay which was nothing but a piece of the Atlantic Ocean, and the Ocean and the river had been fighting at the Bar for thousands of years, the river to get out, the ocean to get in.

"Jeepers creepers now! Look at that!" shouted a tall lad at the tiller of one of the school's cutters. "Look at that black ketch, fellows—*there's* sailing!"

The lads who formed the whaler's crew rested a moment on their oars, and watched. The black ketch, still under the same plain sail, had passed the Outer Buoy and was now shaping a course to come in across the Bar, despite the seas which were breaking almost all along it. The entrance into the little port was not so much across the Bar as *through* it. The Atlantic took a great delight in knocking down the arms of sand which the river-water threw up as a sort of protecting arm against its great adversary, and each time a sand-bar was knocked down, the river picked it up and deposited it some other place. And so there was such a labyrinth of bars and isolated pieces of sand left behind in the tussle, or waiting to be moved into their proper places, that the sea among them was boiling with anger, spiteful and vicious, as if it was the plaything of some bad-tempered giant.

There *was* a channel through the mess, though if the boys hadn't known it they would never have believed it. The channel ran now this way, now that—along a place where the sea had scoured the sand away, and then across the shallowest part of the Bar for a moment, and then again through another hollow with a piece of the Bar one side and another long and untidy arm at the other. Over all this the Atlantic was curling up in great combers, menacing and snarling, and flinging its hungry waters upon all the sands so that it looked quite impossible for anything to live there—*anything*, even a fish.

To sail through, a ship had to remain manageable with the sea doing its malignant best to fling her either upon the Bar, or across it and on the sands alee. It looked hopeless....

"Aye, lads. Better keep her head to tide—it's still flooding—and hang around here a while, case there's corpses to be fished out of this here sea," said a quiet dark lad in the bows.

"Is it as bad as that, Taff? You don't think he'll make it?"

The lad addressed as Taff stared gloomily at the shrieking water on the bar. The whaler itself was safe enough, for the water was almost still in the river, where she was. Taff was a handsome boy, about sixteen, with regular features and a frank, open face. Now he looked like an old fishermen.

"Bar's bad," he said, after a while. "No, I don't think he can make it....But if anybody can, *he* can."

In the few seconds while the boys were watching, the big black ketch was racing at the first of the three fairway buoys, which marked the channel. It was impossible to see them all at once, though they were close together. They tore at their moorings with the force of the tide and the hard wind on them until they were lying on their sides. They were supposed to be conical buoys of a distinctive shape, each bearing its name in white letters. But now they were just bits of black metal that showed now and again, one at a time, in the boiling white water. They served to emphasize the peril of the channel rather than to mark it.

But the big ketch was racing fine. Up to the first buoy, and past it in a flash; turning a little to wind'ard then to race on with the spray and the spume flying, and the seas doing their best to send her reeling upon another arm of the Bar: still she raced. A few moments more! Past the second buoy; another change of course; another leg with the breakers hurling themselves upon her! The lads in the whaler could see a mightier roller than its companions come in from sea, to fling itself upon the Bar with all the force and malice of four thousand miles of Atlantic sea behind it. Up, up it roared, racing at the ketch. The ketch was close enough for the boys to see a figure in dripping oilskins bent low over the wheel aft, another in the bows, conning, and a third half-way up the weather main rigging whence he pointed and gesticulated, obviously watching for the last buoy.

The lads breathed a prayer. Only let the big ketch straighten for the last buoy before that roller caught up with her! Just a moment more! Ketch and roller roared. To seaward a darkening on the western horizon showed another hard squall coming up from there, with others to follow.... The ketch lurched wildly, yawed violently: they saw the figure at the wheel struggling with the spokes. Another figure rushed to slack away more main sheet....

Just at that instant the roller caught her. Up, up, up, the counter of the ketch was raised like a nightmare steeple-chaser intent on taking the water-jump head-over-heels—down went her bows, until the water gurgled in the hawse and the bowsprit was dipping the green sea—over she lurched, until she looked as if she would capsize if she was not up-ended.

For a second or two she hung there, carried along by the onrush of the wind and the racing of the sea, with her stern up and her bows down as if the sea was trying to scrape the bottom of the Bar with her forefoot, or lift her rudder out of the water to make her unmanageable.

Now she was only yards from the inner buoy—the last of the channel. The sea broke. The wall of water seemed to flop down around her and her counter fell back with a sickening crash that sent her bows flinging out of the sea, until her forefoot showed and her bowsprit pointed to the grey heavens. Alee and aweather the breakers roared and crashed and thundered and snarled, and the roller went dashing into the Dovey to set the whalers dancing there and carry away some pleasure craft from their moorings, miles away.... The big black ketch came racing in, past the inner buoy, into the river.

"Whew! Made it!"

The watching lads let out a sigh of relief.

The ketch was racing at them, now.

"Down mains'l! Lively, now!"

They heard the shout as the reefed mainsail aboard the ketch began to shake and spill and then to thunder as its folds were loosened, and the lowering gaff brought it down. The ketch raced past them, still running eight knots and more under only the mizzen and the stays'l. The tide which had been running in four knots was quiet now. It was the top of the tide. For a moment the waters hung there, content, or at least locked in armistice, and for a very brief second or so, the thunder on the Bar was a little quieter and the clouds of spume and sea-smoke rising there did not rise so high. The blackness on the horizon to seaward had lightened, too. For the moment, no more violent squalls were breeding there.

The boys took to their oars to get the whaler back to the jetty, now the ebb had begun. There was some danger that they might be swept out through the Bar channel, out to sea. It *had* happened.

As the ketch raced past, a man aft threw them an end of line to use as a tow-rope. The bow-lad caught it, took a turn quickly, and the whaler began to race astern of the ketch towards the safety of her berth.

"*Warspite*, London," they read on the shapely counter of the big ketch.

"Why, that's the ship we're to sail in," said the lad who had first spoken. "*Warspite*—that's the school's ship."

"And didn't you know that, now?" said the boy called Taff. "Indeed to goodness, what other ship do you think would come racing in here like that now, Yank!"

The ketch was under stays'l only now.

"Leggo the line, lads! Leggo! I'm fetching up here," an oilskinned figure shouted to them.

They had barely time to cast off the tow rope when, with her stays'l fluttering down and her wet canvas thrashing, the *Warspite* turned on her heel and the cable rattled at her bows. She was safely at anchor a stone's throw from the little wharf, and to seaward the Bar smoked and fumed in impotent anger.

"She's come in to take the first watch, my sons," said Yank, who was acting as coxwain of the whaler. "I wish it was us. Boy, I'm looking forward to a run in that ketch."

2

The Maintop Watch

THE boys in the whaler were the Maintop watch of the Outward Bound Sea School. Let us have a look at them as they bring the whaler smartly to her moorings by the wharf at Aberdovey. They had been together a little less than a week and, like many of the hundred boys on the course, they had come from many different parts of the United Kingdom and from Europe, and beyond. The Outward Bound School was famous, and boys came to it sometimes from the ends of the earth.

There were a dozen boys altogether, all dressed in plain blue worsted trousers and blue jerseys, with sea boots and oilskins to keep them dry. Whether they came from the most exclusive schools in England or had been barrow-boys on the London streets ten days earlier, they were all dressed alike. Actually, three of the lads were cadets from well-known school-ships, and two others had already been to sea. In the bows was a sharp-featured small chap who looked about twelve. He was a cadet in the school-ship *Conway*, and was nearer sixteen than twelve years old. His name was Edwards. There was another lad from the *Conway* who was a month or two younger than Edwards, though he was nearly six feet tall and well-built in proportion. His name was Donaldson, and the boys called him Tiny Donaldson. He was a cheerful lad with an affable countenance and arms on him like a young bull's hind legs. He wasn't all brawn and nothing but brawn, by any means. Tiny Donaldson had a good head on him, and had already been elected Captain of the watch. He was expecting to graduate from the *Conway* at the end of the term, and was already promised a place as cadet in the Alfred Holt motor-ship *Calchas* in the China trade—if he had a good report from the Outward Bound, of course.

The other cadet was a superior type—or at any rate, he tried to *look* like a superior type—by the name of Laurence Cholmondeley-Jones, which he pronounced Chumlay-Jones. The boys called him Chum. Chum Jones attended a nautical training establishment at a place called Pangbourne on the banks of the Thames, and it was only the fact that his prospective employers, the Anglo-Saxon Petroleum Company, insisted that its executive cadets should do a sort of trial run at Aberdovey which brought him on the course. Chum Jones was going to be a tanker captain, as soon as possible—according to himself, well before he was 28—and he regarded the Aberdovey interlude as an unnecessary delay. He was a good chap at heart, and he was fitting in very well with his watch-mates.

Another of these was an Irish boy, who was an apprentice to some mysterious rite in a great brewery at Dublin. His name was Mike O'Leary, and he was on the course because his employers thought it would help to make the full man out of him, and a breath of the fresh Welsh air would blow away the malt and the hops from the indoor work at the brewery, for a while. Mike was a happy-looking chap with a quizzical face and a cheerful way of looking at things. His particular mate was a Welsh boy called Taffy—Taffy Davis from Nevin, in North Wales, who was a galley-boy in the Blue Funnel ships, but he was hoping to shift to the deck department the following voyage. He didn't want to be a sea cook.

The Maintoppers were a more than usually assorted collection of maritime and non-maritime youth, even for the Outward Bound. Others in the watch included a hefty young fellow from Iceland who was in England because his father was something in the Icelandic diplomatic service. The boy's name was Hans Beowulfsen. He was so fair that even his eyelashes were white, so white indeed that they were hardly perceptible. There was a boy from Quito, Ecuador, whose name at the school was Pete but at home had been Pedro Henrique dos Santos de Cordoba. Pete was 18, and his father was on a year's business visit to London. Others in the watch were an apprentice from a famous catering firm in London, who went by the name of Curly Mathieson, a chap from a metal-working company in Birmingham whose name was Johnny Shrivenham but who answered to the name of Brum, and a dark little chap from Manchester, Nicky Senussian. A couple of red-headed lads completed the watch. One of these was Don Wiggins, a farmer's boy from Oxfordshire, and the other was the watch vice-captain, Yank. Yank's name was Harvey Brown and he was there because his father was top brass in the U.S.A.F some place in England. Yank went to school at Eton, and this was a month's break to build him up again after an attack of the mumps. Harvey Brown was called Yank on the same principle that Taffy was called Taffy, for every American is a Yank in Britain. It made no difference that he came from Georgia and was not a Yank at all.

So there they were, a dozen lads of all sorts, the only things they had in common being physical fitness, a common age of about 16 to 18, and the plain blue uniform of the Outward Bound Sea School. Yet it was an extraordinary thing that, though they had been together so few days and the Merioneth scene was new to all of them, already they worked together as a team, and liked it. They had settled in amazingly well. Most boys did that. From the early morning shower or dip in the river – whichever was the colder – through the long days of outdoor activities to a big supper and a good night's sleep at the end, they lived full and happy lives. The few rules of the school bothered nobody – no smoking, the observance of proper training discipline, self-discipline under their own elected watch-captain and watch vice-captain. They remembered what the Warden – an active merchant navy officer, like nearly all the staff – had said at the impressive signing-on ceremony in the big hall.

"Lads," he'd said, "I want to welcome you, and I want you to know what you've come to. You're outward bound here. You might wonder just what that might mean. You're outward bound to life, and our month together here is just meant to give you a taste of—well, real living. This is a course for enterprise, adventure, action. We hope you'll find all those things here. But we don't lay them on for you. We can't lay them on for you. We put the school in the surroundings of mountains and sea, where such things belong. We provide the ships and the boats, and the canoes and the mountain trips, and all sorts of real activities, like coast-guard duty, and fire-watching, and beach rescue parties. What you get out of it is up to you. We've been called a school of adventure, and perhaps we are that. But the real adventures have to come out of yourselves—out of the self-discovery by you of yourselves. So we're a school for *self-discovery*, and that's the greatest adventure of all.... Maybe some of you won't grasp what I'm talking about. But you'll find out, before you leave. What matters here and what matters in living is your own self, and that's all—your true self—and the whole point of our sailing and mountaineering and athletics and everything else is to develop that.... We've a badge for those who make the grade. It's called the Outward Bound badge, and I think it's worth having. I hope you'll all qualify. We've a special silver badge for outstanding fellows, but we don't generally award more than one or two of them in a year. And we get a thousand boys through here in a year."

They'd all taken the oath, then, and signed on. The oath was a simple one. A chap just went up to the ensign-covered table, looked the Warden fairly in the eyes, and, giving his name, undertook to become a candidate for the badge, to keep all the conditions, and to work in good fellowship throughout the course.

The whole thing had grown up in the early days of the second world war, when far too many seamen's lives were lost in lifeboats because—too often—the men were accustomed only to work in big ships, where the motion was comparatively slight, the quarters reasonably comfortable, and the work often not actively concerned with real seafaring. They were good crewmen but they were not always seamen, and they hadn't an idea how to look after themselves or anybody else when they were cast adrift in a small boat on the North Atlantic, or anywhere else. So an enterprising Liverpool shipowner and an educationist had begun the sea school to teach young fellows how to muck about in boats. It did so well that it was kept going and indeed extended, after the war. Most boys like mucking about in boats, and the school thrived. A boy did not need to want to go to sea to be taken on. All sorts of boys could go to the course, and they were all welcome.

There was a watch officer in charge of each watch. He was usually a young merchant navy officer having a brief spell ashore, and none of them stayed at the school very long. There was a constant succession of these young fellows who came straight from the bridges of their ocean-going ships and brought the tang of the sea with them—the real sea and the real seafaring. When they showed the boys boatwork and sailing, it was at once obvious that they were not discussing theory. They knew what they were doing, and the boys responded splendidly.

The days sped by. Athletics, pulling the whalers, sailing on the broad estuary, turns at coastguard duty, scrambling on the cargo nets and the monkey-ropes rigged in the tall trees, lifeboat drill, throwing the javelin—activities such as these filled the hours. The fresh clean air, the beautiful Welsh scenery, the tang of the Atlantic breezes and sheer delight in what they were doing, made the boys feel fine. The hundred or so lads at the school were divided into eight watches, and each watch vied with all the others to have its pennant hoisted at the masthead. The watch with its pennant up was that which had done best at the general activities the preceding day.

It was amazing how easy and pleasant it was to learn about sailing, and map-reading, when these things were made real. But the high-light of the course, for most of the boys at any rate, was the run outside in the Irish Sea, in one of the ships belonging to the school, the *Warspite* or the *Garibaldi*. The watches went in these by turns.

"Roll along, our turn in the ketch!" said Taffy fervently. "Let's get a crack outside!"

"Maybe you'll regret it when you do go," said Brum Shrivenham. "The Irish Sea isn't every man's cruising ground, you know."

"Plenty seasick! Ho-ho, plenty seasick!" shouted the lad from Iceland, grinning as if it was a tremendous joke.

J.M.D.C.

3

Introduction to a Ketch

BEFORE going away as crew of the ketch, each watch was made as proficient as possible by sailing in the estuary. They were also taken down in turns to the wharf to go aboard the ships and learn the ropes before they would have to use them. The Maintoppers went down to the wharf the same afternoon that the *Warspite* had come in. The tide was out then, and the two ketches lay far below the level of the wharf planking. The ketches lay on the outside of the wharf, ready to slip away to sea. Inside were two long tidy lines of all sorts of vessels, between the jetty and the wooden retaining wall of the river – cutters, ships' lifeboats still painted in their wartime grey, sailing dinghies, whalers, and a real coastal lifeboat. This was painted white and green, and it was fitted with the distinctive cork fenders all around the upper part of the hull and the enclosed watertight compartments at bow and stern, which were the distinctive feature of the older type of British lifeboat.

Ashore, the rows of tall houses, many painted in gay colours like houses in Italy, lined the road leading to the railway station of Aberdovey, and the hills behind them looked as if they were waiting for a chance to push the whole road-full of houses across the sands and into the river. Gulls swooped and called. The little seaside town looked welcoming, as indeed it was.

"Garibaldi, Liverpool," read Yank on the stern of a husky black ketch which looked strong enough to sail around Cape Horn.

"The *Garibaldi* here is an old French crabber," Mr. McDermott the watch-officer was saying. "That means she was built somewhere on a Bay of Biscay beach, and she spent her early life earning her living, with three men and a boy aboard catching crabs, and sometimes fish. She has sailed across the North Atlantic many times, to the Newfoundland Banks, in the days when small sailing ships went across for cod and brought them back in salt. She escaped from France when the Germans over-ran the country early in the war, and then she was damaged by a fire-bomb in the blitz. Then the school got her and fixed her up. She's a good stout oldtimer with no pretences, and she's easy to handle too – except maybe for that windlass there."

He pointed to a medieval contraption in the bluff bows, where several turns of a heavy iron cable had been taken round the wooden barrel of a sort of man-size winch, and the cable led back along the deck behind the winch.

"Now the *Warspite*," Mr. McDermott was continuing, "used to be a yacht. So that's why you can see at a glance that she's a much slimmer and apparently faster vessel. But she isn't so much faster than the *Garibaldi* as all that. It's the shape of the ship *under* the water that really matters, you know, and the *Garibaldi* is sleek and slippery enough there. Her old bows are like a fish's—they part the water easily and offer little resistance. She can get along. The *Warspite* once belonged to the Royal Naval Yacht Squadron, but she's earned her living through the two big wars. And she's earning her living again now."

"Aye that she is, Mr. McDermott. Good day to you!" called up a cheerful voice from her teak decks, in accents which even Yank could recognise as heavy Welsh.

"Ah, Mr. Hughes. Good day to you! Are you ready for another watch?"

"Aye, that we are! Be so good, now, bring them down."

The boys clambered down the main rigging of the big ketch, jumping the last few feet carefully on to the decks. Yank found himself aboard a thoroughbred of a ship which was even more attractive from her decks than she had been when seen from the pier above. Her teakwork gleamed and her brass glinted in the sun, and the wheel aft and the tall spars were invitations to sail to anywhere.

"Here's a part of the course I can take, hands down," said Yank to Taffy, who looked a little dubious about it.

"Aha, it's seasick I'll be. I'm not used to a vessel like this."

"You get used to it fast. She's a honey! I'd like to see her in the Bermuda race." Yank was enthusiastic. He was sizing up the rig with an experienced eye, following the lead of the gear, and sniffing at a pleasant odour of coffee which was coming through the skylight.

The boys grouped around Mr. Hughes, the mate of

DIAGRAM OF *Warspite*

1 Jib
2 Staysail
3 Spinnaker
4 Mainsail
5 Gaff tops'l
6 Mizzen
7 Wheel
8 Deckhouse
9 Lifeboat
10 Main gaff
11 Main boom
12 Mizzen gaft

the *Warspite*, and listened to him as he expounded on the gear, while Mr. McDermott went down below to get a little closer to that coffee. Beginning in the bows, Mr. Hughes worked his way aft, showing and explaining everything so that even the lad from Birmingham who'd never been near any sort of a ship in his life, soon felt almost at home. The sails were all in their places, but secured, and the *Warspite* was ready to sail at five minutes' notice. Mr. Hughes explained how the sails were loosed, and set, with halliards and sheets, and how the rigging all did its work.

First, he showed everything. Then he had the boys do things for themselves, two at a time to loose the stays'l and the jib, and then the others to set them. Then they hauled the sails down again and furled them—properly, not just a fishwives' bunched-up laundry. After that the whole watch set the big mainsail by hauling on the halliards, peak and throat, until the varnished gaff swayed high aloft. Some went to one side and some the other, and Mr. Hughes, who seemed to have an eye for such things, immediately grabbed the two *Conway* boys and Chum Jones to tend the lifts, where the canvas could be chafed and damage done if things were not seen to properly. Yank went to the head of the throat halliards, which was another post of responsibility, and he soon showed that he, too, knew his way about a vessel.

They set the mainsail and lowered it again, stowing the big sail thoroughly, making the canvas up neat and trim with a fine outer skin on it.

"Things have got to be done right, aboard here," Mr. Hughes was saying. "Now that skin there, you'll wonder why I'm such an old fusspot, now? Couldn't you all just bundle the canvas up, and get the gaskets around it? The gaskets are those lines you're putting round the sail. But you cannot do things like that. Leave a fold of canvas showing to a gale and the whole sail'll blow out on you, in a half a minute. No, no, my lads. Thorough's the word! You'll be crew here, one day soon. Now you mark my words, my sons, and learn while you may, for she'll be jumpin' and leapin' once she gets outside that bar, and half of you'll be feedin' the fishes."

The boys heeded him, and they were willing pupils.

"If anyone'd 'a told me back in Brum even last Saturd'y that I'd be pullin' my guts out aboard a boat like I am now, why, I'd 'a laughed my guts out at 'em. Indeed I would!" said the Birmingham lad, Johnny Shrivenham. "Funny thing, it's work, but you don't mind it!"

And he jumped from halliard to halliard, and downhaul to sheet and lift tackle, at the mate's bidding. So did the others, and Chum Jones was over-heard to remark that it was a 'jolly good show, chaps' no fewer than seventeen times, even before they all trooped down below to look at the quarters there, and have a brew of tea. By that time they felt that they had a real idea of how the sails were set and controlled.

The *Warspite* was as neat and compact below as she was seamanlike and shipshape on deck. As Mr. Hughes said, there was a place for everything and everything in its place, and stayed there unless it was being used. Every single thing was obviously designed to remain where it was, and to perform its proper function, even if the ship were standing on her head. From the twelve-bunk forecastle for'ard—there was a high-sided pipe cot for each boy—to the little engine-room and the sail-locker aft, the ship was a model of neatness and utmost use of space. Next to the forecastle came the saloon, a pleasant cabin done in white and gold with old-fashioned plush seats along each side, and a neat array of sideboards, lockers, and shelves, with a big skylight overhead bringing in the sunshine and the air, and two small ports on either side which were very securely fastened. Off this saloon, on the port side, was the galley, and they all took a look in there. Brightly polished pots and pans hung from a deckhead which also sprouted outsize mugs and coffee-pots, and all the plates and utensils were stowed in lockers so contrived that even if the ship fell over, those plates would stay where they belonged. The stove itself was a patent one, in bright chromium and enamelled metal, made by famous makers who advertised that their stoves could cook at all hours and were most economical with fuel. Taffy, the galley-boy, and the apprentice from the London caterers were greatly taken with the cooking arrangements.

"I wouldn't mind having a go in there," said Curly Mathieson, admiration in his eyes.

"Well, maybe you'll get your chance," said Mr. Hughes. "A boy each watch does the cooking, indeed now. But it's few we ever get that can do the job, or want to."

Two long wooden tables took up most of the saloon,

for all hands ate in there—the regular crew of the *Warspite*, which consisted of no more than three men, the Master (who was away just then), the Mate, and another Welshman who ran the engine and helped to run the ship when the boys were not aboard—and the boys themselves. Yank gathered that the idea of carrying so few men was to ensure that the boys not only formed the real crew but *felt* they did, even though they might be aboard only a few days.

Also in the saloon were some photographs of a big Cape Horn ship, which the Mate was very proud of—"Yes, I've sailed in ships like that," he admitted in response to questions. Across one white bulkhead ran a motto, picked out in letters of gold. Yank read what it said.

TO SERVE, TO STRIVE AND NOT TO YIELD

The boys milled about, filling and overfilling the saloon. They clambered up the companion which reached the main deck through the little deckhouse where there was a bunk for the master, some fire extinguishers, an axe, and a standard compass. Abaft the saloon were the cabins where the officers slept; behind these, the engine-room, and the sail-locker. In the engine-room was a little man with a large engine all in pieces, and the little man was muttering to himself in Welsh. At least, Yank asked if it were Welsh.

"Welsh?" said Taffy. "It is Welsh indeed—wild Welsh that man is talking. He doesn't seem to be very pleased with something—the engine, I'm thinking now."

"Well, she can sail," said Yank.

"She'll need to, my boy, with this misuse of old metal that's called an engine down here," the little man shouted up. "But I'm not knowing what's to get her out across the bar.... Engine, is it...." He spluttered into Welsh again.

"If she ever needs that in a hurry, she's going to need a good crew," was Yank's summary of the mechanical situation after a good look at the engine, which he thought must have been one of the first marine engines installed afloat. Mr. McDermott, coming up at that moment, quite agreed. It was not the *Warspite's* engine that got her anywhere, he said: but its function was merely to help her a little now and then, to see she kept her schedule and was able to get all the boys to sea. With eight watches, and a month only for all to go out, the ketches would have to be off the bar every three or four days to embark a fresh watch.

As the boys formed up and swung along the road again bound for the big house among the hills which was their school, and the Welsh boys led in song, Yank found himself thinking about the *Warspite* and the sail they were to have out in the Irish Sea, and through his mind continually ran the words of that motto he'd read in the saloon, like the chorus of an endless song—

"To serve, to strive and not to yield"—aye, she'd call for service, if it blew up a gale, and she looked the sort of ship that would not yield.

4

Out in the Lifeboat

THE following days, for many of the boys, were the most interesting and, in a curious sort of way, the most satisfying that they had ever spent. From the tingling cold shower at crack of dawn and the morning run until the time they fell into their bunks by night, life was full, fit, and stimulating. Cobwebs were swept away in the keen Welsh air. Swinging up the monkey-ropes and along the taut mooring-line became almost child's play. Sailing on the estuary of the Dovey in the ship's lifeboats, pulling the whalers, making bicycle and foot trips into the hilly hinterland and going for scrambles on the lesser mountains — these were interspersed with sessions of necessary lectures, all to do with the practical stuff of the Outward Bounders' course. Boat knowledge, rule of the road at sea, local conditions (which could be fierce and dangerous), map-reading, simple pilotage, the theory of sailing, a bit of compass work, and sea terms — there were lectures on all these.

Yank began to feel that he had been a member of Maintop watch all his life, and so did the others. The cycle trips in the hills, the commando runs on the mountainsides, getting a heavy boat aground on one of the many sandbanks in the estuary and getting her off again, doing his turn at the coastguard lookout—it was a real coastguard station, and the boys helped to man it—or taking his turn at fire-watching, it was all enjoyable.

Every possible moment was spent afloat. Sometimes there were wild days when westerly or south-westerly gales blew right into the river and a tremendous sea broke on the bar, which no ship could stand, and all the beaches along by Borth and north past Towyn were a maelstrom of white water and swirling sea, and the wind howled about the little wharf as if it wanted to blow the very rail tracks from it.

On such days there could be no sailing, but there was always seamanship to be learned in the comparative comfort of the big shed with its fascinating array of sea gear—anchors, masts and yards, cordage and grapnels of all sorts and sizes, a brace of varnished dinghies, a carpenter's shop where a wizened Chinese from a Blue Funnel ship made blocks and repaired woodwork, a big sail loft, and, pervading everything, that most satisfying odour of stockholm tar and marlin-stuff that reeks of the real sea. An old Welsh bosun ruled the shed. He was a taciturn ancient with keen blue eyes, shaggy great eyebrows of the same fair shade as the Icelander's, and long whiskers growing from his cheeks which looked tough enough to pull out and use as nails. His gnarled old fingers had the strength of marlinespikes, and his very breath seemed to smell of stockholm tar.

When he was in a good mood, which was not always the case, the bosun regaled the boys with yarns of the local sailing-ships, the brave schooners from the Dovey and the little clippers from Portmadoc, up the bay. He'd spent a lifetime in Portmadoc ships, carrying slates around the world, taking salt from Spain to Newfoundland and bringing salted codfish back to Greece and Italy. He spoke of the little ships as if they were persons, and to him Portmadoc was the centre of the universe. Now, his contempt for a sea full of powered vessels was so great that he rarely went away from the wharf except to sail in the Newquay lifeboat. In his deep blue eyes there was always the image of some lovely barque like the *Pride of Wales*, or brave little Western Ocean schooner like the *Blodwen* and her kind. The disappearance of such ships from a heedless world he put down entirely to the machinations of the appalling English, who had – he said – built up great steamship lines and hogged the trade of the world, until there wasn't as much as a hundred tons of slates or a hold full of codfish that a brave Welsh schooner could carry anywhere. Ah, those English! The old man spoke English as if he resented having to use the language, and he used every possible Welsh word and Welsh name that he could. He flatly refused even to speak of the Dovey or Aberdovey. The river was the "Dyfi" and the town "Aber dyfi" to him.

But it was on the fascinating history of the Dovey itself – or his version of it – that the boys loved to hear the old bosun talk. He needed a crony or two from the Cape

Horners or the Portmadoc ships really to bring him out on his own seafaring days, and such cronies were scarce.

"Roman ships came here, boys," he'd say, "and ships from the great Spanish Armada, and ships with the saints from old Ireland. And the great Celtic sailors knew this port and the way beyond the bar – aye, and the way across the Western Ocean, too, long years before any Italian ever passed that way! "It is Welsh that land America ought to be, for it was Welshmen that first sailed there."

He never produced the evidence on which he based this claim, but no one contradicted him. He was on surer ground with his stories of the Roman ships, and the Roman camps and roads, and the Armada ships, and the pirates.

"There were lead-mines all round here, and plenty of cargoes for the ships from the Tiber and the Thames," he'd go on, "and great patriots of Wales came here to hold their assemblies, and muster their men. There on Borth sands, across the river – it is called the *Traeth Maelgwyn* to this day – the warriors met. There was no Norman conquest here in Wales, you'll know! It was here that Cadwgan and Owen took ship for Ireland, to hide a while until it was time to come back and bloody the English nose again. A hundred sailing-ships and more sailed right out of this same Aber Dyfi, now, and the half of 'em were built here, right near where you're all a-sitting! And the fisheries were enormous. It was great times, indeed; it was great times...."

The old boy's voice would trail off as if he still were listening for the rallying shouts of the men of Cadwgan

J.M.D.C.

and Owen, or hearking to the sigh of the trade wind in an outward-bound barque's rigging. Yank felt himself transported back a thousand years. Who on earth Cadwgan and Owen might have been he didn't know, but Taffy told him they were great heroes of Wales.

When it came to getting the lifeboat ready for a run to sea, the bosun did not spend time in reminiscences. This was the last pulling and sailing lifeboat in Britain, and it had been given to the school when the Newquay boat was replaced by a power-driven vessel. Only when conditions were such that the boys could be brought up quickly to a high pitch of efficiency or the weather remained particularly good throughout the course, was it customary for the big lifeboat to go outside. She was a difficult craft to handle for any but her old regular crew.

She was sailed with a rig which was rather awkward for novices, and her oars were long sweeps rather beyond the power of a boy. The Maintoppers were delighted when Tiny Donaldson told them they had been selected to take the lifeboat for a run outside the bar.

Even the old bosun almost approved of the Maintop watch. The boys were mostly big lads, and the watch included more than the usual proportion of youths who came to the school with some sea training already behind them. They were just the group to handle that lifeboat. The Old Man himself—the Warden was always called that—took charge, with Mr. McDermott the watch officer along with him, and the boys took a day's food and a blanket apiece, in case they were unable to return the same day. Once you took a ship through the Dovey bar, unless you came more or less straight back in again on the same tide, there was no knowing when you might be able to sail in again, and the lifeboat needed quite a depth of water to float her, even with her center-boards hauled up.

By this stage, the boys were so accustomed to the sailing precautions that they took them as a matter of course. All wore seagoing lifejackets of varying patterns, and these were adjusted before they got into the boat and pushed off from the wharf. They went out on the top of the tide, going down the estuary under oars. The passage through the bar began only about half a mile from the wharves, and they had to be ready for it. At slack water, the lifeboat approached the bar rapidly. The boys pulled like experts, which was more than they had done at the beginning of the course. The orders by now had a familiar ring, even to the lad from Birmingham.

"Fix stretchers."

"Ship crutches."

"Oars ready!"

"Toss oars."

"Oars down!"

"Give way—together!"

And off went the graceful white and green boat like a swan, while the boys lifted their eyes now and again to admire the loveliness, yet once more, of the setting of the little seaside town. It was a gem of a place on a day like this, with the sun shining and the wind quiet. The estuary was a broad silvered sheet with the river at high water, and all the sands were covered for an hour or two. The big iron refuge stood up incongruously, like a raft on stilts, and the port seemed to have acreage enough to anchor a fleet of liners. But there was still a roaring on the bar where the breakers were.

"Conical buoy ahead, sir!" shouted young Edwards, on the lookout; and another buoy, and another, came into view, jumping in the swell. Now they were in the channel, among the sandbanks of the bar, and Yank wondered how the old tops'l schooners and brigs and barquentines were able to negotiate the place. The channel led first this way, then that, going right between long lines of sandbanks which even at the top of high water glinted yellow and white so close by. In places the channel could be wide enough barely to allow a ship to pass, without touching the bank. For a stretch of about a quarter of a mile, it led actually between two lines of sandbanks, with the sea making over them and the swell coming from the southwest causing a set on to the inshore bank, to the grave peril of large vessels without ample power. In the channel itself there was a smooth area, but this was only comparative. Before the boat was half-way through, the tide was racing on the ebb and the breakers set up a sullen roar as they felt the opposition. Soon the boat was tossing like a piece of jetsam in a surf, and the Old Man at the tiller was having his work cut out to keep the lifeboat to her course.

"Handsomely, my boys, handsomely! All together, now: backs into it!"

Mr. McDermott himself was stroke, pulling as if he loved it, and the Old Welsh bosun had joined young Edwards on lookout in the bow. To some of the lads, with the dancing of the boat and the great exertion, for a moment or two Aberdovey itself seemed to be dancing, too, and the line of high houses did a crazy hornpipe against the blue and green hills. Now the stern of the boat rose high as the tide raced past and the water swirled angrily at the channel-marking buoys, and the roar of the breakers was menacing and constant.

"Handsomely, lads! Not far to go now."

The Old Man was smiling, eyes puckered up, an expression almost of exultation on his face showing his delight to be handling a sleek boat and a good crew, bringing her out into the open sea from the confines of the land.

Buoy one, buoy two, buoy three rushed past, and the boat leapt in a tumble of foam. Once a great comber like a Cape Horn sea swept at her and seemed determined to crash into her, bringing her to permanent grief. But she rose like an albatross upon the breast of the sea and took the wall of green water in her stride.

"That's it, my lads! That's the way. Keep good way on her, keep her going."

A few of the boys were feeling somewhat green about the bows themselves, for it was the first time they had made the passage through the bar and felt the violent motion there. But the keen fresh air and the fine sea wind, filling young lungs, and the delight in good team-work, kept them from the more active forms of sea-sickness, at any rate for the moment.

"Ah, there's the fairway buoy now," said Mr. McDermott, as a buoy with a topmark, larger than the rest, came into his field of vision, abeam. Almost at once the motion quietened. The boat was through the passage and over the bar. The long lines of green water flinging themselves, one behind the other like marshalled lines of watery hills massed to attack the land, were not half so menacing when seen from the seaward side. Line after line of water which approached the coast quietly until it felt the challenge of the bar, rose into long walls, up and up and up, curling and snarling, to hurl themselves upon the land of Wales as if they wanted to wash it all away.

"Oars!" came the warning.

"Toss oars!"

A dozen long oars leapt aloft, wet blades glinting in the sun and the water dripping.

"Unship crutches!"

"Boat oars!"

The long oars came inboard, to be stowed neatly and securely fore-and-aft, out of the way of the sailing-gear. Already the lifeboat was well clear of the disturbed water round the Dovey bar. There was a gentle breeze from the west-south-west, and the masts had been stepped before they left the wharf.

"We'll give her her canvas and go for a sail," said the Old Man. "Just the day for it, too," he added with satisfaction.

It was not until the sails were hoisted aloft and set with perfection on the two stout masts that the boys had time to sit down for a moment, and notice the view. The lifeboat slipped along effortlessly and almost upright, the blue water of Cardigan Bay lapping at her white sides and the blue sky above looking as if it never had been any other colour and never would be again anything but a glorious Mediterranean blue. The boat sped northwards about a mile or so from the land, which came down to the water there in a sweep of sandy beach with a railroad at the back of it and, beyond that, the mountains of Wales. Yank had never seen North Wales from the sea before. The old bosun just sat in the bows, staring at it. The glorious valleys and the beautiful mountains made a perfect scene. Away in the north-west the horn of the wide bay was lost in the haze of Bardsey Island, where the saints of Wales were buried: to the north, on the starboard bow, was great Snowdon, highest mountain of them all: just for'ard of the starboard beam was Cader Idris, looking like a gentle mound of the land of Wales lifted up to feel the life-giving warmth of the sun.

Yank stared and stared. He'd heard of the Bay of Naples, of Rio de Janeiro, even of the beauty of the distant Bay of Islands in New Zealand where his father went fishing once. But why had no one ever told him of this lovely Cardigan Bay off Wales? The place was perfect.

"That's Bird Rock up there now, boy, and the Bwlch there now, and Corlan Fraith, and Taren Cwm-Ffernolm. Yonder town ye're seein' by the foreshore there is Towyn, and to the north of that comes Barmouth. You'll be seein' Criccieth and Criccieth Castle, and Harlech Castle, and all the grandest hills of Wales before the day's done...."

He lapsed into Welsh poetry, and Taffy the galley-boy took up the refrain until Chum Jones put a wrench in the proceedings by suddenly sitting up and shouting that it was a jolly good show and absolutely a wizard back-drop.

"Jolly good show?" said the old bosun. "I'll have you to know it's no show you're looking at! That's Wales! And him with the good name of Jones," the old man muttered, looking sadly at the boy, as if he failed to comprehend how anyone with the good Welsh name of Jones could have become such—such an Englishman.

The lifeboat sped along before the slowly freshening breeze, while the day continued perfect and almost every moment brought fresh vistas of the beautiful coast. They passed the Bwych buoy, and if the name had not been painted on it in very large letters, Yank wouldn't have had the faintest idea how to spell it, or pronounce it. They passed by Barmouth, and high Cader Idris, well inland —it looked a mighty mountain to run up, as Curly Mathieson remarked—and then stood away from the land to round the end of the Causeway, that long arm of rocks that reaches into Cardigan Bay.

"It's all drowned land around here," said the bosun, whose version of history was always picturesque if not wholly accurate. "Yon Causeway was the stone wall of a Welsh landowner in these parts, and the sea rushed in one day and took his fields. The fishermen out of Pwllheli fish up strange things, to this day. Though some say the rocks got up in the sea for the saints to walk on, to Ireland."

Whether the Causeway was a rockway for saints or the drowned wall of some ancient Welsh giant's field, Yank didn't know, but the water boiled around it even on that fair day and, here and there, eddies raced and the sea showed a swirling surface, indicating a profusion of foul bottom close below. On one place were the remains of a steel ship. The Old Man gave the buoy a good berth. "Causeway," it said as if everybody reading it would know which causeway it was. It was a larger buoy than the others, and a bell clanged slowly and mournfully on it as it rolled slightly in the sea. A large cormorant looked disdainfully at the lifeboat as it sped past, and the bosun shouted at it.

An hour or so more and the boat was dancing past St. Tudwal's Roads, with the horn of Trwyn Cilan and all the Nevin peninsular aweather. Now it was Taffy's turn to grow lyrical, for he was born at Morfa Nevin round the corner. After a vain but moving endeavour to rhapsodise on the history, beauties, and paramount perfection of all North Wales, Taffy and the old bosun lapsed first into Welsh, then into song, and then, finally, into an eloquent silence. Indeed it was all a lovely place on such a day, seen from the silent and graceful little vessel. Past St. Tudwal's, eastwards they spun, the boys taking turns at the tiller under the Old Man's eye, while Mr. McDermott and Curly handed out the lunch. Lunch consisted of great slabs of brown bread with corned beef between. "Fishermen's slices," the Old Man called them – none of your ladylike stuff – and all hands fell on them with a will. Yank could hardly manage to stretch his mouth wide open enough to get one in. He ate seven.

The boat sped along, past the beach at Pwllheli, past Criccieth and its ancient castle ruins, towards the bar off Portmadoc where the old bosun waved his ancient cap three times in salute, he said, to the great ships which had come bounding out of there, a roll of foam at their cut-waters and the song of the wind in their rigging, all the world at their bows. All this time the Old Man, Mr. McDermott, and the bosun were busy pointing out land-marks, explaining the lay of the land, giving details of the worth to ships—or lack of it—of the various small ports. The holding ground at St. Tudwal's Roads—"I've seen twenty sailing-ships there myself, windbound, all waiting for a slant: and the gay sight when they were all off!" sang the bosun—the depths on Pwllheli Bar, the anchorage off Criccieth: all were pointed out and duly noted by at least those among the boys who intended going to sea. Yank was as attentive as anyone. He declared his intention, "when he'd made some dough," of bringing his own ship over to these waters and going cruising himself. The Old Man had a chart spread on the after-thwart, and they all pored over it.

"We'll make a swing around Tremadoc Bay and have a look at Harlech, and then home for the Dovey bar," the Old Man announced as the afternoon wore on, for it was a long sail. "We'll see how the weather is. It looks settled enough. What do you say, bosun?"

"Aye now, good enough. And I'm thinkin' it'll turn to

the east'ard next. Give's three days of that, and we'll have three weeks."

"If it stays good we'll keep under way. Or put a grapnel down for the night somewhere off Barmouth, or maybe under the hills between Towyn and the Dovey," the Old Man declared.

The evening found them under the grim square castle of old Harlech. "Doesn't your blood sing here!" shouted the old bosun, breaking into "Men of Harlech" in a very loud voice. The breeze dropped a little, though the boat still had good way. The evening was perfect. There were plenty of fishermen's slices left to provide an ample supper, washed down by water. At nine o'clock, watches were chosen—three watches, with the Old Man, Mr. McDermott, and the bosun in charge, and their petty officers were Tiny Donaldson, Yank, and Tich Edwards. Yank's crowd had the gravy-eye watch, from four a.m.

When it was dark, towards half after ten, the lads not on watch rolled into their blankets with their oilskins above them, the bottom boards of the old lifeboat for bunk and the stars for covering. This is the life! thought Yank, as he fell into deep and untroubled sleep, and the lapping of the waters on the planking was a lullaby. Two boys kept lookout in the bows, another had the tiller under the eye of an officer, and the fourth was stand-by.

To them all the old lifeboat was like a Portmadoc clipper reborn, and the high stars seemed to reach down to kiss her masts, the soft black night to hide from her a harsh world beyond the horizon, in which she no longer belonged. To steer, to keep lookout across the dark waters, to listen to the sighing of the gentle wind, to watch the flow of the graceful sails as they imparted way to the shapely hull—to do any of these things was to feel a share in the adventures of the illustrious past. Men of Harlech, Men of Portmadoc, men of all the Nevin Peninsula—warriors and sailors all—their ghosts arose from an adventurous past and sailed through the night with the old lifeboat, with her freight of youth outward bound for life, and the deep sea....

5

Joining the Warspite

IN the soft grayness of a lovely morning the boat came back to Aberdovey, and passed through the bar channel at half-tide with a minimum disturbance. It was always easier to go in than to come out. It had been nothing but a simple sail, yet it had also been a memorable adventure. Everyone from the Old Man down was delighted with it.

"I wish we could get in a run like that with every watch," the boys heard the Old Man saying to Mr. McDermott, "but that Cardigan Bay—" He broke off, with a look astern at the waters which were quiet just then, but very often were not. "Now, my lads, it's the *Warspite* for you next, isn't it?"

"Aye, sir. It's our turn next," said Tiny Donaldson with pleasure in his voice.

"I'm expecting her in tonight or tomorrow morning. You'll have to join her off the bar. She can't get in with these neaps."

Even the most abject landsman among the boys knew well what neaps were, for the neap tides did not bring water enough upon the bar to allow the *Warspite* or the *Garibaldi* to sail in. The ketches needed about eleven feet of water to float in, at least, and that meant that there should really be thirteen feet on the bar to let them come in safely, for the rise and fall of the seas on a gentle day would take two feet of water. Sometimes there would be fifteen feet to float them, and sometimes eleven, which was the bare minimum. So when the tides were low they did not try to come in, for fear of pounding, or worse. Instead, the watches went out in a big cutter, sometimes towed by Ellis Williams with his fine motorboat, sometimes under their own power, and they jumped aboard the ketches as they lay hove-to outside. According to accounts which other watches had brought back, that could be a lively experience.

Next morning, sure enough, the lads on coastguard duty called early to announce that the *Warspite* could be seen, making for the Outer buoy, off the bar. Tiny and Yank had the watch ready. Orders were to take a minimum of gear, their blankets, their oilskins, and food enough for five or six days. Chum Jones' idea of a minimum of gear consisted of every single thing he possessed, and he had come to the school armed with a portable typewriter, a portable gramophone, and two cameras. He'd been told that it was a good idea for a shipmaster to be expert on the typewriter, he explained in answer to Mr. McDermott's amused queries. The officer had to admit that maybe the lad was right. So the portable typewriter went along. The others managed with a seabag between each pair of them. Even so, by the time all twelve and their gear and food, and the *Warspite's* other requirements (such as a few bags of galley fuel and some spare cordage) were all piled into the boat, she was fairly full. Ellis Williams towed them to the bar, with Mr. McDermott in charge of the boat. By now the buckjumping and switchback-riding of the boat in the breakers was familiar. The boys had the oars ready in case the towline parted. Once the boat took a wild sheer when she was passing through that part of the channel where the scend of the breakers was right across it, and she touched on the sand once or twice. Ellis soon had her off, and on her way.

Aboard the *Warspite*, which was dipping and rolling so that half her copper bottom showed alternately on each side, they could see the boys of the watch they were relieving, the Foretop, shouting and waving as they approached. The big ketch was not at anchor but keeping slow way with her mainsail run down in its gear and the mizzen and big fore stays'l set, giving her a speed through the water of perhaps a couple of knots. The lads hanging over the side looked extremely pleased with life, though up in the bows one little boy still hung over the rail with his face very green, and no delight on his countenance whatever.

A section of the bulwarks on the lee side had been removed to provide easy access to the decks, and as the boat approached this, the boys saw the deck was piled high with sea boots and sea bags and bundles of oilskins, which the departing watch was taking off with them.

Now the boat was alongside and the transfer began. It was strange how at once the motion of both boat and ketch seemed to increase tenfold, making everything difficult.

Immediately the scene was one of intense activity. Blue jerseyed boys scrambled aboard the ketch and more blue jerseyed boys scrambled into the boat out of the ketch. Sea bags and everything else whizzed through the air as the boat jumped and the ketch rolled, until Yank couldn't for the life of him understand how things would ever come clear and he half-expected that, when the 'transfer' was complete, the watches would be mixed up frantically and all the wrong gear would be in the ketch. But he soon saw that there was a very real order to the apparent confusion. Mr. Hughes the mate knew how to handle this situation, which was old stuff to him. All the outgoing gear was on the port side of the ketch, grouped neatly by the deckhouse, and all the incoming gear was flung at once across clear to the starboard side, so there could be no confusion. Indeed not as much as a nut of anthracite or an Irish potato was dropped, or mislaid. The watch captain of the watch being relieved had a good grip of his boys, too, and the right group of lads descended into the boat.

All this took about three minutes. Mr. McDermott saw to it that the gear in the boat was properly stowed for the run in through the breakers again, and Ellis Williams was back alongside in the twinkling of an eye to tow the boat. The Maintoppers each gave their life jackets to the lads going in, and took life jackets from them for use in the ketch. In less than five minutes since the boat came alongside, she was off again, the Foretoppers giving the Maintoppers a good cheer of farewell.

"Hoist the mains'l!" was the order aboard.

Yank found himself at the wheel while the other boys, under the keen eye of the Mate, went to the foot of the mainmast and took hold of the throat and peak halliards there. The Mate was everywhere at once, tending the sheet, seeing the lee lift was slack so the wire would not chafe through the canvas, and the weather lift taut to support the boom, encouraging the boys, seeing the gaff went aloft swift and clear. The boys hauled with a will, a *Conway* lad at the head of each line, while the *Warspite* fell away on her course and began to steady, with the greater area of canvas to keep her listed in the growing breeze.

"Steer NW¾W," said the Captain to Yank. "Know the compass, lad?"

"Aye, aye, sir! NW¾W," repeated Yank, in the approved manner, like an ancient mariner and, with a spoke or two, he brought the ketch to her course. The wheel was light and easy and she obviously handled like a witch.

"Have you been at sea, then?" asked the captain, when Yank's turn was over.

"I've been on a Bermuda race, sir," said Yank.

The captain looked at him. Though he had been at sea all his grown life, the captain had only a vague idea as to what the Bermuda race might be. He seemed to recollect that it was a hard affair of slogging a group of small yachts from somewhere on the eastern seaboard of the United States down to the island of Bermuda, across the Gulf Stream and through all sorts of adverse conditions, driving the yachts night and day and making what was often a very difficult landfall at the end. He had a deal of wondering admiration for anyone who would deliberately seek a tough piece of sailing like that, and call it sport.

"Bermuda race, um? Was it tough?" he asked.

"Not too bad, sir. The Fastnet can be worse!"

"Been in that, too?"

"Only once, sir. But I'm hoping to crew again this year."

The old captain took a quizzical look at the red-haired lad. As an old sailing-ship sailor himself, he was glad to know of these ocean-going yachtsmen who kept the spirit and the art of sailing alive. The captain was a grey-headed man grown old in the service of great cargo liners in the trade to China and Japan and down to Australia. The *Warspite* was by far the smallest vessel he had ever been in in his life, by at least a thousand tons. He'd begun his sea career at the turn of the century in a shapely little Scots barque. All her sort were dead and gone, long since, but he had qualified in them. He was glad he had, for it had served him in good stead throughout his long career and through two world wars.

His reflections on this subject were cut short by the Mate's report that everything was secure and all things in order, the boys' gear stowed down below and the twelve bunks properly allocated. This was done by the watch-captain, Tiny Donaldson. Not all the bunks were alike nor even of the same length. They all had the main requirements for a tolerable rest at sea in a small vessel—

they were fore-and-aft (that is, along the line of the keel) and they had high sides to keep the boys in if the ship rolled violently, as she certainly would.

"Muster the watch, Mr. Hughes," said the captain.

"Muster aft, boys. Lifejackets on!"

The boys made their way to the open space by the wheel, some of them staggering a bit, for the *Warspite* had a big deck with room enough to throw them off-balance. It was different in the life-boat, where they had had to stay where they were. In the ketch there was room to walk. They had to find their sea legs.

The captain stood aft where all the boys could see him, and explained to them briefly a few necessary things about the running of the ship. They would, he said, be divided into two sections, to be called the port and starboard watch of the ketch, the port under the vice-captain and the starboard under the watch-captain. The boys were the crew of the ship, and there was no other crew. He relied on them, and so did the ship. There were a few simple rules to be borne in mind, such as no talking to the boy at the wheel, no crowding on deck and no unnecessary congregrating abaft the mizzen-mast, fresh water to be used sparingly, no ports to be opened (because of the danger of swamping, even in good weather), and so on. The captain explained each of these rules, and why it was necessary. Then he took the boys over the vessel and showed them the fire-fighting gear, the pumps, the spare sails, and once again, the running rigging.

Then they were divided into the two sections, which were as follows:—

Port	*Starboard*
Yank	Tiny Donaldson
Taffy	Hans the Icelander
Tich Edwards	Mike O'Leary
Pedro de Cordoba (Pete)	Johnny Shrivenham (Brum from B'ham)
Curly Mathieson	Nicky Senussian
Chum Jones	Don Wiggins

This made two well-balanced teams.

"Now we'll take a sail first up to Abersoch, and we'll put her through her paces a bit so you'll get the hang of things on the way," the captain concluded. "We'll probably put the anchor down in St. Tudwal's Roads for the night. You boys had a long day yesterday and you'll have a longer tomorrow, for we'll be away at first light and make a long board down to the Tuskar, or maybe run through Bardsey Sound and make across for the Codling or the Kish lightship, and sail around them and back again. Or perhaps into Dun Laoghaire, by Dublin, if the conditions are good. We'll be out a couple of nights then. So we'll take it a little easy today and you'll get a rest this night, I hope. We'll have sandwiches on the way to St. Tudwal's and a good hearty meal when we get in. There'll be anchor watch tonight from 6 to 6, each boy an hour. Watch-captain to draw lots and report names to the mate. Now, do you all understand everything?"

"Yes, sir!" came the chorus.

"Fine, then. Mr. Hughes, we'll begin instruction at the wheel."

Each boy in turn came to do a trick at the wheel, steering the ketch under her full suit of sails. She was running easily, making about five or six knots, but poor Brum Birmingham and one or two others had a bit of a job at first to decide which way to put the wheel when the ketch got a little off course. Old Brum, for the life of him, couldn't get the idea and tried to bring the lubber's point back to the compass-course he was supposed to be steering, with the result that the ship got more and more off course. But Mr. Hughes saw she did not take a complete turn round.

"There's fierce rocks here, sonny," he said. "Now do you see yon buoy, the Sarn-y-Bwch? Well, watch that and don't let it swing all over the place. Put the wheel the way you want the ship to go—like a car, now. Indeed to goodness, like a car!"

At these magic words—"like a car"—old Brum really felt at home, and rapidly became one of the most expert helmsmen. It was with the greatest reluctance that he left the wheel at all, to hand over to Pete who promptly had the ship heading somewhere towards Peru. But they all got the hang of it, in due course, and though her wake was like the tortuous track of an outsize snake, somehow the *Warspite* wandered on her appointed way towards St. Tudwal's. Bwch buoy came abeam, and course was altered to allow good sea-room for passing the Causeway well outside, NW. by N. it was, and NW. by N.—more or less—they steered. The weather was fine and clear, the breeze light south-west, and the sea slight.

"Too good to last, sir. Too good to last!" Yank overheard the Mate saying to the Captain.

"Well, we'll use it while we can. We'll tack her and wear her and jibe her round, so the boys will understand what's going on. Ready about!" shouted the captain.

"Ready about!" echoed the Mate.

"Ready about!" shouted the boys.

Again the lads mustered aft, and the Captain explained to them, in a few clear words, just what he was going to do. A sailing-ship, he said, could not always go the way she wanted to go, but she could get where she needed to be by beating. That simply meant zigzagging against the wind, first this way and then that, gaining in the desired direction each time, until her objective was reached. The process of getting her round from one direction to the other—the zig to the zag, so to speak—was called tacking, or wearing, and it meant simply that from sailing as close as possible into the eye of the wind on the one side, she did the same thing as quickly as possible with the wind on the other. She tacked when she was put across the wind, right into it (and for that she needed fair speed and good weather): she wore round when the weather was bad, and in that case, she ran off before the wind and jibed on to the other tack—that is to say, swung the sails across carefully when the wind was behind her, to bring the wind on their other side. It was all quite simple, but it had to be done properly without doing any damage, or putting strains on gear which it was not designed to accept.

First the Captain showed the boys how the ship could make any number of courses, by putting the wheel first one way and letting the ketch run off, easing the sheets of the main and mizzen as the wind drew further and further aft, and then jibing the booms across—letting them go on a controlled run, with the gaffs and the sails swinging from one side to the other—so the wind was on the other side. The boys saw that the ship could sail almost round a circle, but there were a few directions in which the wind made it impossible for her. Unless the sails were reasonably full of wind they could impart no forward motion to the hull, and when the wind was nearly ahead, the canvas shook so much that the sails were useless.

They had gone over all this in lessons on theory of sailing at the school, of course, and they had tacked the cutters and the small yachts in the estuary of the Dovey.

When everybody had the hang of what was happening with the ship as she was put through her paces, the Captain said that it was time to go about—to 'make a board,' he called it. The Mate stationed the boys, instructing them in their duties. Yank went to the wheel, and glowed with pride to hear the Captain say, "That boy has a nice touch with the helm—there must be something in this ocean yacht-racing." Tiny Donaldson stood by the backstay, the Mate explaining that his was the important job of keeping the mast properly stressed, and his duty was to slack the lee backstay, run across the deck, and set up the stay to wind'ard as the ship came round. Tich Edwards went to the lifts, Hans the Icelander took charge of the boom tackle on the main, and Chum Jones took the mizzen. Taffy, Brum Shrivenham, Mike, Curly Mathieson, Pete and the rest were disposed where they would be of most assistance, and the Mate himself went into the bows, taking Don Wiggins with him to look after the head sheets.

Then all was ready, and the big ketch boomed along with good way and all the gear clear for running, every boy at his place.

"Lee oh!" shouted the Captain; and Yank put the wheel down spoke by spoke to bring the ship into the wind without losing her way, not slamming the wheel down but treating it gently, as the bows and the long bowsprit swung towards the open sea with a rush, and the sails began to slat and bang. The boys had been well instructed. The jib sheets were let go when the wind came ahead, and the backed stays'l canted the ship's head further until the wind had swung right across the bow and began to take the big sails on what had been their lee side. Over went both booms, over went the head-sails — all three of them — sheets and tackles were set up heartily, weather backstays and lifts attended to, and in 59 seconds flat, timed by the Captain's stop-watch, the big *Warspite* was round and bounding along on the other tack.

"Good work, my lads!" beamed the Captain. "Ten minutes on this tack, and see if we can do it again in 45 seconds."

So they beat and beat, until the *Warspite* was spinning like a top and every boy was near perfect at his drill and, not only that, understood all that was going on as well as his own part in it. They changed jobs until each felt that he'd a good grasp of the whole thing. Then they wore the ship around, which took more time and lost her some ground, though she came up to the wind again very quickly. Jibing had to be done carefully lest the main-boom took charge and caused damage. Indeed, everything had to be done carefully and properly.

"That's what a sailing-ship is for and that's why you're here, lads," the Captain explained to them. "Most countries in Europe, and the American Coast Guard, keep big barques and ships just for this reason—to bring boys up right in the ways of the sea. You can fool with a steamer perhaps, but things must be done right in any sort of a sailer. You start right if you get the hang of working a ship at sea. Now we'll practice Man Overboard! Any volunteers? For the boat, I mean; we'll not want anyone to jump overboard!"

They all volunteered to man the boat, which was carried slung outboard at the davits, always ready. A lifebuoy was dropped in the water to simulate a boy and the ship manoeuvred across the wind to take the speed from her, while the boat was lowered with the utmost speed and the buoy picked up again. The morning and half the afternoon sped past without anyone having time even to admire the glorious Welsh scenery.

At last the order was Belay all, and the ketch was put on her course again for St. Tudwal's Roads, while Curly Mathieson and the little Welsh engineer (who'd been busy all day trying to get a lighting set to function properly) disappeared below to get a good stew cooking in the galley. Soon delightful odours of a generous stew came floating up through the skylight, while the islands off the Roads danced into closer and closer view—West Island, with a big white lighthouse making it conspicuous, and St. Tudwal's Island to the east.

"Keep Garn Nevin well open there, between the point of Wylfa and West Island," was the order to the helmsman as the ketch ran steadily onwards towards St. Tudwal's Sound. To young Edwards at the wheel, the cliffs seemed dangerously close as the ketch ran between them and the rocky island. He could see some seals sunning themselves on the inshore rocks, and the sea was swirling along the base of the high cliffs. The scenery was grand and wild and the little bay of Abersoch looked most inviting.

The mizzen and stays'l were run down, the ketch making for her anchorage under main and jib. Mr. Hughes was for'ard again, looking to the anchor. Aft the Captain stood by the wheel, conning. Once in the Sound, most of the motion went out of the sea, and the ketch ran on in an almost ghostly silence broken only by the wash of the water on the nearby rocks, and the screeching of the welcoming gulls. Hans the Icelander was sounding with the hand-lead and the Welsh engineer had his head up from the open skylight of his beloved engine-room, to admire the view, or perhaps to sniff the stew.

An old lifeboat shed on a point came abeam.

"And a half three!" sung the Icelander at the lead.

"Bring her up a point," to the helmsman, from the Captain, who motioned with his hand to indicate with certainty the way he wanted the ship to go.

A small yellow house peeped out behind the lifeboat shed.

"And a quarter three!" from Hans.

"Down helm! Stand by to lower the main!"

A second or two. A great shaking of the sails, the ship coming to an orderly halt in her stride. And then:

"Let go, Mr. Mate!"

"Let go it is, Sir!" And the best bower fell into the still water with a splashing and a running out of cable.

"Two shackles in the water, please, Mr. Hughes."

"Two shackles in the water, Sir!"

Now the ketch swung head to wind, and the big mainsail was taken in, like the folded wing of a big sea-bird. Everything was made shipshape and orderly, the decks swept and washed down, the riding light made ready, and the boys trooped down below to an enormous meal of glorious stew washed down by large cups of tea, with slabs of some hearty sort of cake called 'afters.' At any rate Curly said it was cake, and it made good ballast. The boys ate together in the saloon with only one on watch on deck. The Captain sat at the head of the starboard table, and the Mate at the port, and many were the questions fired at them. How long the boys might have gone on yarning and talking there was no saying, but towards 8 o'clock, the Captain called a halt.

"Now, my lads. To your bunks, except the anchor watch. It will be a long day tomorrow."

Aye, a long day tomorrow – there was little doubt about that.

6

Driven Off!

"SOME miserable poaching skunk from Aberdaron has been here," said Mr. Hughes, shaking his head sadly as the crayfish pots came up empty. "And this the best spot for crays in all the Roads."

It was the crack of dawn, and the *Warspite*, her engine and its ancient chain-drive rattling busily away, was close in under the rocky sides of St. Tudwal's Island at a special place where Mr. Hughes was accustomed to put down crayfish pots. He had been a fisherman out of Pwllheli, when he was not in the deepwater ships, and he knew every crayfish hole and every rock round all Cardigan Bay. It was the ship's custom to pick up the pots when there was a chance, and this was a good moment for it as she was off on her way for a good sail. But there was nothing in the pots, and no bait either.

The weather did not look very promising but there rarely was any promise in a Cardigan Bay dawn, except of bad weather. Even in the shelter of the little island, which lay well in round the corner of the Roads, a slop on the sea made the ketch dip and roll, and there was a wet sighing in the wind that boded no good. While some boys were getting the pots up, the others went for a scramble ashore to pick up gulls' eggs on the peaty island summit. There was a flat stone to land on, and a rough path led to the top. It was a queer place, and though the holiday hamlet of Abersoch was just across the Roads, the boys felt that they would not like to be marooned there. They had time only for a quick scramble, and then back aboard with a bucket half full of eggs. The *Warspite* lay about her own length from the rocks, but she was quite safe. The boys were aboard quickly.

"We'll back out," the Captain said. "Go astern!" This he called down through the skylight to the engineer. There was an awful row going on in the little engine-room, with much clanging and rattling of metal. Yank looked down in some mild alarm but was partly reassured to see that most of the noise came from a long endless chain which was rushing round at the for'ard end of the engine. The *Warspite* was built as an ocean-going yacht before the days of good auxiliary engines, and had never been intended to have one. So she was not properly fitted with a propeller driven from an engine. Instead, an ancient paraffin engine had been installed at some time in her long career *above* a propeller shaft, and the shaft—and so the propeller—was turned by a system of cog wheels and a chain drive like a bicycle wheel. The chain rushed around, the cogs rushed around, and the propeller rushed around too, sometimes. The engine drove the chain and the chain drove the propeller, and the engine was old and weak and the propeller was small.

"Full astern!" shouted the Captain, blowing three short blasts on his whistle at the same time.

"Full astern, Sir!" shouted the engineer, almost covered with black oil.

There was the most terrible noise from the engine-room. The engine coughed and spluttered and there was a commotion as if large pieces of metal were being exploded from it. Metal clashed on metal. Sparks flew. Black smoke poured through the exhaust in the ship's side. Then the engine began to race. The ship, which never had had much appreciable sternway, came to a stop.

"Hoist the stays'l, Mr. Hughes!"

"Stays'l halliards, my lads. Lively now!" The big stays'l for'ard was hauled aloft in a matter of seconds.

The engine meantime was stopped and the little engineer, his face blacker than ever, appeared at the coaming of his teak skylight with a length of chain in his oily hand.

"It is the chain drive again, Sir," he announced more in sorrow than in anger.

"Well, we'd better go back to anchor now and you slip ashore and get it fixed at the garage," replied the Captain. Trouble with the chain was obviously nothing new. "Is it any worse than usual? You can fix it, I suppose?"

"Its an awful mess. But it can be fixed. But what we're needin', Sir, is a new engine altogether."

The Captain stroked his cheek. The ship could manage quite well under sail alone, though the engine was undoubtedly a great help when going through bar passages, and keeping away from the Causeway and out of trouble generally. Engineers always wanted new and bigger engines.

"I'm not liking the look of the weather," said the Mate in the Captain's other ear. What a pair of pessimists! There was plenty of evidence in support of the Mate's remark, for the grey morning was anything but promising. Overhead, wherever it was clear, already the high scud was flying, though the official forecast was good enough.

From St. Tudwal's Island to an anchorage in the Roads was a short distance, and with the stays'l run down, the black ketch was soon anchored again. Before the boat could be prepared to take the engineer ashore, a small motorboat from the beach was seen coming off. In a few minutes it was alongside. There was only one man in it, a local boatman who acted as a sort of agent at Abersoch for the school and the ketches.

"They're wanting you to come ashore and 'phone the school, Captain!" he shouted as soon as he was within hail. "There's a message for you."

"Keep a good eye on her, Mr. Mate," were the Captain's parting words. "I agree with you about the weather, but it is probably only local. It happens so often here, you know. Give her plenty of cable if the sea starts rolling in, and watch the forecasts. I'll be back as quickly as I can. The cones aren't up yet."

The Captain and engineer jumped into the motorboat which was away ashore with them without loss of time. The Captain's remark about the "cones not being up" was a reference to the official gale warning signals. If a gale was expected, signal shapes made of canvas in the form of cones were hoisted at the signal staffs of all the coast-guard stations, and one such staff was in clear view from the ship. The boys watched the boat make for the entrance of the little river, and disappear round the bluff headland by the yacht club. An uncomfortable lop was already coming into the Roads, and the wet sighing of the wind had noticeably increased. It was poor weather, undoubtedly, but not exactly bad—as yet.

"We'll close-reef the mains'l, and look to the storm lashings of everything, my boys," said the Mate. "There's nought like being prepared."

He looked a little grim as he said that, and Yank noticed that all the time they were shaking out the canvas and putting in the double reef, Mr. Hughes kept looking out to sea towards the south-west, as if he expected a hard blow from there at any moment.

"You don't think the ship's safe in these Roads, Mr. Hughes?" Yank asked.

"No ship's safe in Cardigan Bay anywhere, my son."

"But there's shelter here, surely, from anything but south to east?"

"There's good shelter from winds from S.W. right around through west to N.E., aye. But the wind often sets in suddenly with freshening squalls that come from south. The winds seem to funnel in the Bay. Ah-ah, I'm not liking it, indeed I'm not!"

"Is there a safe anchorage we can make for, if it did come on to blow a gale?"

"There's Pwllheli. It's the only safe place around here. But we're neaped out of there—neaped out of everywhere! There's too little water in these tides, and they're all bar harbours. You know, made by rivers. Rivers build up bars at their mouths or spill sand down somewhere to get in the way of ships," Mr. Hughes explained. "We'll shift anchorage when the Captain comes back, and make her snug. She'd do all right just behind the island, but we'd need power to get her there. He'll be bringing back the chain."

The Mate spoke quietly enough, but he kept looking at the weather. There was no sign of the returning boat. Mr. Hughes said it might take hours to fix the links. It was early in the morning and the forge would have to be started.

Now to windward it was obvious that a heavy squall was making up. How heavy? Large drops of rain began to fall. Mr. Hughes paced up and down by the wheel, now looking somewhat anxiously towards the beach whence no boat came, now to seaward, where anything might be brewing. The anchorage where the *Warspite* lay was not the one she had left, earlier, and she was somewhat exposed to the wind blowing in. Further in, in line with the lifeboat house, there was a better place.

Mr. Hughes made up his mind in a very few moments. He'd take the ketch in there without further ado under sail.

"Heave up, my lads! Heave up! All hands to man the capstan!"

"All hands man the capstan!" was the instant response. The boys were ready. The cable was led round the capstan in the way that it should go, the fore stays'l and the mizzen were loosed and ready to set. Two boys jumped below to stow the chain in the locker beneath the floor boards of their quarters, as it came in. The rest took the capstan bars and began to tramp round the small capstan. Steadily the cable came in, link by link.

"Heave lively, my lads! Lively, now!" The Mate struck up an old capstan song he'd learned when he was in the big Cape Horners. By this time the rain was coming down in torrents, which now and then shut off the view of all but the nearest land, and the wind was freshening steadily.

"Heave, and break her! Heave, and she must! Heave, till you bust!"

Straining at the capstan bars, the boys heaved and heaved, for the holding ground was good just there and the anchor clung to the mud.

"Get the stays'l and the mizzen on her. Yank, you go to the wheel. As soon as you feel she has way, keep her up. We'll get to wind'ard a bit and see what happens. It mightn't be too good to get in by that point now. And the open sea's the safest place for us."

The sails thrashed and boomed as they were being hoisted. The boys were glad the big area was already shortened by the reefs they had tucked in earlier.

With the reefed mizzen and the fore stays'l aloft, the ketch broke the anchor out herself. Yank watched carefully at the wheel, for she was leaping like a broncho.

"Now, lads, get the anchor up and secured!"

The *Warspite's* anchor had to be lifted up to the rail and lashed there. It was not the stockless type. This meant heavy work. Mr. Hughes led the way, with Hans the Icelander and the two *Conway* lads and Chum Jones close at his heels, the others following. Getting the anchor secured in a seaway was not easy, but they managed. As yet the force of the sea was not running into the Roads. No sooner was the job done than a temporary clearing of the rain showed more ugly squalls racing in from the North Atlantic. Perhaps they were local, but they certainly looked as if they had come a long way.

"We'll plug about here until the Captain comes out. Then we'll get her snug into a hole behind the island. I know just the place. She's been there before," said Mr. Hughes. "We'll be all right, my lads! Now for a bit of a sail."

The Ketch was plunging along, a cloud of spray at her bows. But it was soon obvious that the tide was carrying her inshore—too close inshore. There was not much water for her there. The sea was breaking at the foot of the cliffs by Llanbedrog.

"We'll have to set the main," Mr. Hughes, standing by the wheel, speaking almost to himself. No trace of anxiety was evident in his voice. "All hands to set the mains'l!" he shouted.

Again the boys ran to the halliards, Mr. Hughes at the head of the line.

It was when the gaff was half-way aloft that the accident

J.M.D.C.

happened, as quick as a flash. Mr. Hughes was working like a dozen men, setting a magnificent example and exhorting the boys to the utmost effort, his great arms flailing at the halliards and his mighty voice booming out the musical sailing-ship calls to set the rhythm of the work. With the gaff half aloft, something jammed. He ran out quickly from the foot of the mast to see, and just at that moment the jammed gear freed, the halliards parted, and down came the peak, hitting him fairly across the head. If the gaff had not been hollow, Mr. Hughes would have been killed.

As it was, there was the Mate stretched unconscious on the deck, a trickle of blood slowly oozing from beneath his cap. The ship was leaping and rolling, the gaff was banging and the sail was making a noise like breakers thundering on the beach, and, nearby and to leeward, that very sound itself added to the tumult. The breakers now were thundering upon the beach with a vengeance and the big ketch was driving upon them, without way enough to claw off. Yank at the wheel caught a glimpse through the murk of a boat trying to make for them from the river, but it could not catch up.

At the precise moment the gaff halliards carried away, the wind came down like a blow from an avalanche, and roared across the water in a smoke of spray and spume. The *Warspite* staggered. The very force of the wind, for the moment, kept the sea down, and the ketch raced. The stays'l and the reefed mizzen were canvas enough just now! The boy at the wheel kept the ship to her course, steering her with the utmost care though she was over almost on her side and the conditions were alarming. Where could the ship go? Still she was being set alee despite her apparent speed through the water. Yank tried to remember from the chart the lay of the Bay up there—Tremadoc Bay. To wind'ard somewhere—and not far, he remembered: indeed, perilously close—were the treacherous rocks of the Giant's Causeway or St. Patrick's Causeway, whatever it was called. God help the ship if she got on them! To leeward—aye, now, what was there? No harbour! Nowhere to run! He remembered all too clearly Mr. Hughes saying that—neaped out of everywhere, no place to go! No water on the bar at Pwllheli which was so close by, and safe, if only the ship could be sailed in there: no water on the bar of the river off Portmadoc, and heaven help the ship if she were set down upon those grim rocks off there. The whole of Tremadoc Bay was a terrible lee shore and the rocks of the Causeway made the arm of a great trap which pinned them in!

"Tiny! Hans! Get the mains'l down! Get some gaskets round the sail before it blows out!" He called to his watchmates. The Icelander and a group of the boys had got Mr. Hughes temporarily into the lee scuppers, where he lay unconscious and, for all they knew, dying. They whipped some lashing round his inanimate body to hold him for the moment, and jumped to get the gaff secured and then the sail, which was blowing about like the side of a circus tent in a hurricane. Tiny Donaldson showed himself well worthy of his selection as watch captain. Getting down the gaff was no easy task. Again and again the canvas of the mainsail broke out of their grip as they tried to fight it down. The rain continued pouring and every boy was thoroughly wet through. The roaring of the wind in the rigging was a noisy challenge, and they worked like demons.

Even so, it must have taken the best part of an hour to get the gaff properly down and the sail bundled up in its gaskets, with a good stow and a tight skin so it would not blow away again. Three times it had blown out. Thank heaven for the reefs in it! The full mains'l would have been unmanageable.

As soon as the sail was reasonably secured, Tiny fought his way along the reeling deck to the wheel to confer with Yank.

"This looks like being one of those unforgettable experiences they were telling us about," shouted Yank above the noise of the wind.

Tiny grinned.

"But where do we go from here? She's being set towards the beach all the time, and already we've lost a lot!"

"*That's* the question. We'll keep her up with the sail she's got on at the moment. First thing we've got to do is to get Mr. Hughes down below where he can be comfortable. But I don't know how bad he may be hurt."

"He was only hit on the head. I mean, nothing internal, or anything like that."

Tiny seemed to think that a blow across the head even with a flailing gaff was the sort of thing any old sea-dog should be able to take in his stride.

"Tiny, you take the wheel a moment and I'll have a look at him—not that I know the answers."

Yank chose a moment when the ship was lurching in the right direction to fight his way across to the lee bulwarks, where poor Mr. Hughes lay bundled up in a piece of line, in an oilskinned heap. The trickle of blood from his head wound had stopped. At least he had some colour, and appeared to be breathing. It was going to be immensely difficult, getting him down below. Meanwhile the wind was increasing and increasing until it was blowing half a gale, and its direction varied from S.S.W. to S.S.E. Yank fought his way back to the wheel, where all the boys had gathered. Taking Taffy, he went into the companion-way to have a look at the chart. The night compass in there was lying over at a crazy angle.

"I don't like the look of this chart. Look at it! The whole place is littered with 'Hell's mouths' and 'Devil's Tails' and other nice names, and it's all the lousiest, rock-filledest, dangerousest hole I ever did see! How are we going to get out of this, with the wind forcing us into its worst corners?"

"Beat out," said Taffy. "That's what we have to do. We'll have to beat out of Tremadoc Bay anyway, and then hope for the weather to improve. Ships have done it before, you know. They had to, whenever they came out of Portmadoc."

Beat out? But the violent wind and the set of the tide were forcing them nearer and nearer to the farthest leeward corner of the bay. Taffy peered through the glass sides of the little deckhouse.

"I've seen us drive by Pwllheli," he said. "And Pen-y-Chain. And Criccieth now cannot be far away. Maybe we could get a lee under Criccieth Castle. *Maybe*. But I doubt it. We'll have to have a go at it if she continues down to leeward like this. Or get the mains'l on her. Think she'll stand it, Yank?"

"Looks like she'll have to—the close-reefed main, anyway. Let's get those halliards spliced and rove again. Hey, Tiny! Hans! Chum Jones! Give's a hand to fix the main halliards!" Yank dashed out on deck with Taffy at his heels. Tiny was struggling manfully with the wheel trying to keep the ship up to the wind, with the cold sprays and the wild spume breaking all over her. Yank shouted to him what he proposed to do and the lads fought their way to the foot of the mainmast, Mr. Hughes forgotten for the moment. The great job was to fix the halliards so the sail could be set again. Unfortunately, the boys found that the halliards had parted where the hemp line was married to the light pliable wire, of which most of the hailliards were formed. It was a difficult job of real sailoring to marry the two parts together again, the more so as the *Warspite* was trying to play leapfrog with the wild sea. Time and time again she flung the boys down in a heap on the deck. They fought their way to their feet again, only to be flung down once more. The galley funnel went overboard like a feather in a gale, and the sails were wind-stiffened like sheets of armour-plate. Sea, spray, and rain wet them through and through. But the lads stuck to the job. Yank and Hans the Icelander knew a little about splicing and so did the *Conways* and Chum Jones, but none of them had any experience of this kind of thing.

Just as the last tuck was being made Taffy looked up and pointed through the murk of flying spray.

"Criccieth Castle!" he shouted, as the grey ruins on their solid cliff showed in a temporary clearing, with a line of grey houses inland back of the cliff and a wall of white water breaking at its foot.

A glance showed Yank that there was no hope of shelter in the lee of that cliff. There was no lee. The great breakers were flinging themselves everywhere along the rocky beach.

"We'll have to get the peak of the main up and beat her out now, fast!" Taffy shouted. "There's only a mile or two to go before she's on Portmadoc Bar!"

But it was almost impossible to get anything set. The violent wind, ever freshening, was determined to roar at all their efforts like an angry demon, waiting to dash the ship on the rocks in the corner of the bay and grind her to matchwood. If that happened, no one was going to swim away. Yank knew that full well. The trouble was that in those conditions of wind and tide and violent sea, the ketch could not fight to wind'ard out of the trap with only the reefed mizzen and the storm stays'l set.

"That sail must go aloft," said Yank grimly through clenched teeth. "Come on, boys! Aloft with her—peak first! Away, now! Together! Long and strong!"

They missed the Mate's strength, even though they took the throat halliards to the capstan with four boys heaving on the bars there, and the rest of them tallied on the peak halliards. Slowly, slowly the bulk of the big main fought its way aloft. Time and time again it seemed that their efforts would be useless, or the sail would blow itself out. But it had been sewn well. Thank the Lord for that! It did not blow out. Cloth by cloth, inch by inch, they fought it up until it was set at least well enough to give some useful driving power to the ship.

It was only then they looked and saw the roaring tumult of the sea upon Portmadoc Bar, close alee! Within a matter of moments the ship would be matchwood unless she could hold her own. Hold her own? She had to fight to wind'ard, too! And then? The line of cruel rocks of the dreaded Causeway was right in her path!

"Lifejackets, my lads," said Yank, in as quiet a voice as he could use in that howling wind. They'd forgotten them, earlier. As far as he could see, the ship had now no chance at all. She had been set down too far to beat out again now.

"Cross the Causeway! Cross the Causeway!" The shout was in the Cape Horn voice of Mr. Hughes. "Cross the Causeway! There is a way!"

7

Across the Causeway!

"THERE is a way!"

The words galvanised the boys into action. The ship, too, seemed to be gathering way. Maybe the tide was changing; maybe she could claw off! The boys ran to the place where Mr. Hughes was lying in the scuppers. They found him, very white, peering over the rail in the direction of the grim mountains behind Portmadoc. Tiny Donaldson and Mike O'Leary held him up. Hans the Icelander was at the wheel, where he obviously was an expert.

"The – only – way – out – of – this – lee – corner," Mr. Hughes spoke with the utmost difficulty and seemed to be fighting to remain conscious, "is – to – cross – the – Causeway. I don't – know – if she – can – make – it – at all – with – this sea. Get – me – to – the – wheel – where – I can – see...."

The boys threw the Mate's lashings off, and dragged him carefully across the deck. It was not far, but with the ship's bucking and lurching and jumping, and the constant sprays and heavy water breaking over her, it was a very difficult job. *Everything* was immensely difficult–

getting the lashings off, steadying Mr. Hughes to see he did not fall, getting him across the pitching, reeling, soaking decks. Once or twice while they tried, he lapsed into unconsciousness again. But at last they managed.

Meanwhile the ship was snoring along on the starboard tack, heading somewhere south right towards the Causeway. As soon as he heard there was a passage there, Yank had shouted to the Icelander to give the ship a little way and let her go off the wind slightly. But the infernal wind was hauling west and west-south-west in ever-freshening squalls, as if it was determined to force the ship on to the lee shore before she ever had a chance of trying her luck with the Causeway.

Mr. Hughes looked up again, and peered into the murk astern.

"Even with this tide and the water banked up with the wind, it's a chance," he muttered. They bent close to hear what he said. "She *might* make it.... But I've got to be able to see!... There's marks. I'm looking for Moel-y-Gest...."

"Who the heck's Molly Guest?" asked Yank in bewilderment.

"A hill," Taffy explained. "It's a hill ashore he's looking for. *Moel*, hill. It's a Welsh word."

"I want to see Moel-y-Gest," said Mr. Hughes, "and Moel Hebog back of that.... Taffy now, boy, do you see them?"

"I don't know Moel-y-Gest, Mr. Hughes. It's from Nevin I am. I've never been this way before."

"Moel-y-Gest and Moel Hebog in line. . . . That'll bring us to the channel east of the Causeway. Bring me the glasses, lad, and hold them for me."

Six boys rushed for the deck companion where the ship's binoculars were kept, glad to know they were an exceptionally good pair from a captured German submarine.

Mr. Hughes peered at the murky outline of the nearby coast long and hard. Sometimes he gesticulated feebly with one hand, signalling to the Icelander at the wheel to fall away from the wind a little, or to come up. Astern the murk was thick, but now and again the boys could see the loom of the hills, and sometimes the dim outline of a big hill by Portmadoc and the mountains beyond in the Snowdon foothills.

"I've got Moel Hebog, Mr. Hughes!" Taffy shouted excitedly. "I've got Moel Hebog!"

He pointed somewhere astern in the grey rain.

"Aye, lad. And yonder's Moel-y-Gest. Steady as she goes, there! Steady—as—she—goes!"

"Can I ease the main sheet a trifle, Sir, to give her better way now? Seems like the wind isn't drawing any more ahead." Yank asked anxiously.

He had the situation well sized up—too well, maybe. From the furthest leeward corner of grim Tremadoc Bay the coast of North Wales trended south by Harlech and by Morfa Dyffryn towards Barmouth way. Once the ship was over the Causeway—if she did get over the Causeway—she would at least have room to manoeuvre, for a while. The wind was forcing her towards the rocks all the time, but she had a deep keel and a fine hull, and she should hold her own now the sails were properly set. So long as they stood! He looked up at main and mizzen, but so far at any rate they were all right. There was not a sign of a split or a parted stitch anywhere though the strain on them was terrific. The ship was burying her black bows into some of the turbulent steep seas and throwing heavy water half-way up the mast, as she fought her way along. Easing the mainsheet even a trifle would help. She would sail faster then; soon it might not be necessary to keep her right up into the wind's eye as high as she could go.

"Hold everything yet a while! Don't start anything," said Mr. Hughes. "When we get among the breakers—then, maybe...."

Among the breakers! Why, of course there would be an absolute turmoil of boiling, maddened sea all about the Causeway rocks, miles and miles and miles of it. Only a perfect ship could live through such a sea!

It cleared a little astern. Thank heaven for that, at any rate. Taffy and Mr. Hughes got good bearings from the hills they were keeping in line. Moel-y-Gest and Moel Hebog—a much higher mountain further inland—kept in line astern of the ship, would lead her to the place where there might be water enough to let the ship fight across the Causeway. It was not a real channel. It was the place where the rocks dropped lowest below the surface. There might be eighteen or twenty feet of water, in some places. But it all depended upon the force and the height of the breakers—and the ship could be overwhelmed in the horrible breakers, too, even without being dropped upon the rocks and pounded to pieces.

"Secure – everything, Yank.... Make – sure – no – water – can get – in – or – the – seas – will – swamp – her...."

Mr. Hughes was weakening again. His head fell forward, his eyes glazed.

Yank had seen to the companion ways and the skylights before, and everything was as secure against water as it could be made. The doors of the small deckhouse were closed and the canvas covers were over everything. Some water found its way below, of course, but no dangerous weight of sea was yet down there, or even on deck, for the big ketch rode like a racehorse, a thoroughbred steeplechaser taking a series of difficult fences. She rose to every sea as if determined to escape its wrath and leapt towards the next, and the next, and the next.... But they must be approaching the Causeway now. The seas rose higher, higher, higher! The wind roared. The water flew horizontally away from the wet shrouds and the halliards and every piece of cordage. The bows dipped deeper and deeper as if they were trying to bite the water, angrily. The wake astern streamed back in a wide foam-flecked river. The seas smashed at the bows like great wet sledgehammers. The very mainmast seemed to sway as the ship would lurch violently to leeward and then bring up, all trembling, as if bracing herself to meet the shock of the next wall of dreadful water. The strain upon the weather rigging made the stays hum and sing like a great harp upon which the fiends of hell were playing. To windward now they saw the Causeway. It boiled and smoked and fumed, and the visibility that way was not more than a hundred yards. A hundred yards of such a scene were enough—more than enough! Could any ship live in that?

Hans at the wheel kept the ship to the last compass course Mr. Hughes had steadied him on, with the mountains in line astern. But the compass swung and lurched and jumped just as the ship did, and sometimes it would swing violently through an arc of half a dozen points. None among the boys but an experienced Icelander, indeed, could have held to a compass course just then. To him, keeping a wayward little ship to something like her course was familiar enough, and even a Cardigan Bay gale, off Iceland, would be a summer breeze. Impassive, stalwart, his blue eyes peering kindly from beneath the brim of an outsize sou'-wester, water streaming down his face and down his neck and everywhere, Hans was in control of the wheel, and, indeed, of the ship. Now he had to cling to the spokes lest he be flung right overboard as the ketch stumbled in her headlong stride; now he braced himself, sea-booted young legs akimbo, as she fell in a hole in the sea. The spray tore at him and the spume lashed him and the wind shrieked in his ears and flung its needle-points of spray into his eyes. Beside him, huddled on the teak grating there, was the figure of the half-conscious Mr. Hughes. On the other side, Yank, clinging with both hands to the mizzen rigging. Behind him, the boys, clinging to whatever they could to keep themselves from being blown or flung or washed over the side. Lifelines had been rigged fore-and-aft—for this was regular practice, even in the best of weather—and it was as well they had. It was encouraging in all that tumult to catch a glimpse of the calm face of Hans the Icelander—no tenseness there! Maybe he had not seen the chart. But he could see the breakers, for they were all around.

Now the ship rode in the very breakers, and all the land astern was shut from view. She must keep the compass course, or die! Each time as she flung herself half-buried in the spray into some frightful hole left by a passing sea, Yank expected to hear the dreadful crunch that would tell of pounding. She would pound only once. For those rocks would reach up and smash her as she tried to pass, ripping off her great lead keel, capsizing her in the murderous surf. To leeward the surf boiled and boiled towards the rockbound land. No help there! For all that land was nothing but a death-trap for ships forced upon it, in weather such as that.

The Icelander smiled, smiled to see the way the good ship was fighting for her life. These English could build a ship! Even if she did go down, she was going fighting—and never for a moment did it occur to him that she would lose.... To Mr. Hughes, to Taffy from Nevin, it was perhaps a different story. They remembered well long histories of doomed ships—doomed ships, and drowned men. Not many ships had ever beaten the sea, here: but a few had. Generally they had beaten the sea by running for Portmadoc Bar, which could be as dangerous as beating across the Causeway. The bones of many a good ship were strewn on both.

The moments now seemed hours. Still there came no crunching of keel upon the rock, no fatal, final pound.... The sea was almost burying the ship every time she flung herself forward, and the ketch was halted in her stride, so that her progress became a nightmare leapfrogging with a watery grave at the bottom of each leap. Yet onwards she came, always fighting. Now the boys were one tense group, not saying anything, not hoping anything; clinging there, waiting. Would she make it? *Could* she make it? Could any vessel live in so wild an onslaught of the sea?

There were times when the answer seemed to be a fatal No.

Yet still she did not pound, though the snarl of the rocks must be right below them. Once in a break to wind'ard for a second, Yank thought he saw the granite of the Causeway bared as the sea, having flung itself to a violent height, retreated for a moment to gather strength for the next mad fury. He glanced anxiously aloft, at the wheel, at the half-conscious Mr. Hughes. The ship still kept her steerage way. Not even the most violent sea that swept over her quite halted her.

Nobody sounded with the leadline. There was no use sounding. Either she got across, now she was in the channel, or she did not. How much water was under her keel, if any, was in the hands of God. The answer really lay in how far she fell in the trough. The really important sounding would be made by her keel. She stumbled on,

like a stricken animal, like a great sail-fish fighting the hook, like a wounded gazelle seeking sanctuary before its blood-stream poured out.

Mr. Hughes dragged himself to his feet, staggered to the compass, knelt beside the little bowl, clinging to the binnacle. His cap had rolled off, and blown overboard. His old grey-red hair was mottled with blood and wet with the rain. He peered across the compass card, staring into the murk abeam to pick out some well-known point. Would it never show?

"What is it now?" asked Taffy.

"Moelfre. Moelfre, son. Know it, now?"

"No, Mr. Hughes. I've heard of it, though."

"Its a high mountain between Harlech and Barmouth. We must bring it abeam."

"Ah, there are many mountains here! But show it to me, Mr. Hughes, when you see it. Then I'll keep an eye on it."

"There! I see it! Nearly abeam already.... She's sailing, boy. She's a beauty! She's going to get out of here...."

Mr. Hughes turned to Hans at the wheel. "As she goes!" he shouted, his voice much stronger. "You're doin' fine!"

Again he bent to the little compass card, the wild swinging and lunging of which seemed to disconcert him as little as it did the Icelander. They were a pair, in this sort of thing.

It was blowing as hard as ever, but the rain had eased. Astern the outlines of the hills about Portmadoc were quite clear now, and Harlech Castle showed its stubborn square block huge upon its hill. Moel-y-Gest showed up well enough for all to see. Mochras Point, down on the sea, was lost sometimes in a rage of breaking water. But it was there. Mr. Hughes, gesticulating heavily, pointed it out to Hans.

"Now keep her as she goes on this good course until yon Mochras Point comes into line with Moel-y-Gest," he shouted as well as he could, and Taffy repeated. "Then keep them astern a while, an' she'll be clear. There's other Banks about, but none to worry her once she rides the Causeway here!"

The speech was too long for the injured Mate. Still clinging to the binnacle, his head fell forward and he lapsed again into unconsciousness.

But his work was done. The ketch still stumbled, lurched, contorted madly in an insane field of leaping sea. But the weight of water was gone from her slim decks now. No longer did her bow bury itself so deep as she met the onrush of the seas. The longer, truer sea already was evidence that the worst was past. What might still be in store for her the boys did not know, but she was across. Over the Causeway! Yank sweated at the mere sight of the raging sea astern, now that its most dangerous fury was behind them. The Icelander grinned.

8

Where Do We Go Now?

THE ship might be safely across the worst of the Causeway, but now where could she go? The boys were so relieved to be out of the worst savagery of the sea that, for the moment, they forgot that while the gale was blowing, there *was* nowhere for the *Warspite* to go in search of shelter, at any rate not in Cardigan Bay. They turned to Mr. Hughes, but poor Mr. Hughes had maintained consciousness only by a supreme effort for the passage of the Causeway. Now he had passed right out.

"Let's get the Mate below where he can be out of the cold and the water first," said Yank. "Then we'll worry about what to do next. Keep her as she goes, Iceland."

"Oh-ho!" said the Icelander at the wheel, looking as if there was nowhere on earth he would sooner be. "As she goes!"

The boys struggled to get Mr. Hughes down the companionway and into the saloon. The ship still jumped and lurched and leaped all over the place, though nothing like she had when among the Causeway breakers. Her bows now rose right out of the water and tried to jump into the sky, only to drop again an instant afterwards and try to bury themselves in the depths of the sea. But no longer were they really being buried, nor did heavy water break over the bulwarks and descend on deck. Sprays and spume flew everywhere. To stand at the wheel was like being in the backwash at the foot of Niagara Falls. But it was not now really dangerous.

It took the best part of an hour to get the unconscious Mate below, his outer garments removed, and to put him in his bunk. An eerie light came through the big skylights with their canvas covers shipped. Everything was difficult, almost as if there were some power trying to make things as difficult as possible. Boys stumbled and fell, flung off their balance by the violent motion of the ship. One or two had to run for the companion and dash back on deck where they were immediately and violently seasick, for the motion in the confined space down below, without the fresh sea air, was more than they could stand. But they always came back again. Poor Mr. Hughes' bunk was rather wet too, and the little cabin was damp and cheerless. The boys chocked him in his bunk with cushions from the settee, and hoped for the best. For the moment, there was nothing further they could do, and they hoped that the Mate would come round again soon, in a matter of hours, maybe—at the worst, in a day or two. One was left with him, to keep watch.

Yank, Tiny, Taffy, Tich Edwards, Chum Jones, and Mike O'Leary gathered in the glass-sided deckhouse to peer anxiously at the chart and consult about the best thing to do. It was as much as they could manage to keep their balance in the deckhouse, even sitting down—or trying to sit. Yank had the chart and Taffy was explaining it.

"First," said Tiny Donaldson, "I vote we need a Captain in this ship. My vote's for Yank."

"But what about you? You're watch-captain, aren't you?" came a chorus.

"Yank is the only one among us—except perhaps old Iceland at the wheel there, and we wouldn't know what he wanted us to do—who's been really at sea before in a vessel like this. So Yank should have charge until Mr. Hughes recovers. I'll be glad to be mate. What about it, Yank?"

"Why, fellows, I thank you, and I'll be glad to do what I can. But I don't know these waters, you know."

"None of us do. You *can* sail the ship. I've never been out in a thing this size before. All right, that's settled. Now, where do we go from here? Where on earth can we go?"

Indeed this was a problem. The visibility had worsened again. To leeward sometimes the bleak and awful coast of Wales showed in the stormy murk, but sometimes it was hidden from view altogether and round them everywhere was nothing but the boiling sea, like a scum upon the surface of a dismal devil's brew, all streaky green and grey and dirty white, and altogether depressing. The chart showed that, though the wind was favourable enough to run for Barmouth, they could not get in at that port because there was not water enough on the bar to let the ship run in. The same thing applied to Aberdovey. What a murder of mad water would be raging on the bar there!

Besides, there were more dangers in Cardigan Bay. The Causeway was not the only miserable arm of rocks reaching out to increase the perils of a dangerous lee shore. Off Towyn were the Bwch shoals, and though there might be water enough on them to get across, it would be foolish to get among them if it could be avoided. A ship which had crossed the Causeway in a gale of wind might not have much to fear from the Bwch shoals, but the sea there would be violent and confused, and it was no use looking for trouble.

"I'd like to have a look at Aberdovey so they'd see us ashore, maybe, and at least know we hadn't gone down," said Yank. "But then what? There's *another* lot of no-good shoals and rocks and patches off Aberystwyth south of that—and a bad lot, too. No, we can't get among them!"

"We'll have to keep her on this tack until we get to wind'ard of the whole Causeway, and then wear around and go for St. Tudwal's again," said Chum Jones, to everyone's astonishment.

"Why, that's sense," said Yank, looking at Chum Jones approvingly. "The old Welsh brains coming out at last, eh, now that Wales is trying to drown him!"

They laughed at this, Chum joining. Indeed his was the only practicable course. Yank had hoped to keep the ship sailing towards the south until she was able to get behind the shelter of the long nose of Wales which stretched towards Ireland—perhaps behind the headland at New Quay, or down to Fishguard. But he observed ruefully that the awkward arm of rocks called the Patches, reaching out into Cardigan Bay off Aberystwyth, made such a course impractical. The wind showed no sign of easing. The big ketch could not beat on for ever under so great a spread of canvas, yet she must carry sail to make over the ground. He looked aloft as he thought of this, for the hundredth time that day. The big sails were standing up well, so far, but for how long? The strain was terrific. Going about was *not* going to be funny. Well, they could not stand on, and they would have to go about—and go about, too, without knowing clearly where they were, gale-driven there in the dreadful trap of Cardigan Bay. They were out of the worst of it, yes, but there was plenty more to come.

Yank fought his way out on deck. Somewhere in the murk astern the long jagged arms of the infernal Causeway reached miles across the *Warspite's* path. Somewhere in the murk ahead were two more causeways, minor ones, but dangers nonetheless. And how on earth was he going to find St. Tudwal's Roads again, *if* the ship weathered the western end of the long Causeway? How did you know where you were in a place like Cardigan Bay, when there wasn't a thing to tell you? He judged the ship's speed over the bottom—no, through the water, he couldn't know what the sets and the tides were doing, under such conditions—to be perhaps six knots. She was heading about south, more or less parallel with the coast. So long as she kept on that tack, he *ought* to see something before getting among the foul Patches off Aberystwyth. They were a good twenty miles from the Causeway, as he read the chart. He would have to chance the Bwch shallows.

He made up his mind. He'd stand on that tack—towards the south—until either he saw something identifiable or got among the broken water indicating shoals. Then he'd wear around, and stand on a broad leg towards the direction in which he hoped St. Tudwal's was. They'd just have to see something identifiable up that way, too: maybe the light in the big lighthouse would be showing by then. Maybe it would be dark. Though it would take a mighty powerful light to pierce the dreadful gloom of a south-west gale.

He looked aloft at the gear. That seemed to be standing, all right, though the whole mizzen mast was working with every violent jump the ship made. Some of the boys were huddled round the counter, finding what shelter they could in the lee of the little engine-room skylight. Others were in the shelter of the deckhouse.

He sent Taffy to the lookout and relieved the Icelander at the wheel.

"Coffee?" said Hans inquiringly.

"A good idea—see what you can do!"

They had had nothing to eat since breakfast. Come to think of it, Yank didn't even know what time it was. Already it seemed days since they had hauled up the crayfish pots off the island. He looked at his watch. Twenty past ten, it said.

Hans disappeared below to see what he could do in the galley. Taffy called a couple of the lads to help him on the lookout, on the wise principle that six eyes were better than two on such a day. The ship bounded on. Still nothing could be seen, and the rain threw itself at them as if some Western Ocean giant was playing with the ship with some outsize hose. They should be off Barmouth by this time. Still nothing. There was a bump in the land where it came out towards the west'ard to the south of Barmouth Bay. They'd have to clear that. Perhaps she was doing well enough to keep far out from that land—she'd better be! All the land around that bay, thought Yank bitterly, was nothing but a trap for ships. Well, he'd do his best to see it wasn't going to trap this one. But he'd be mighty glad to get that anchor down once more in St. Tudwal's Roads.

Hours passed. Hour after hour. He was so wet through he wondered whether his skin was still waterproof, and had visions of the driving rain soaking right into his spleen and all his veins. More hours passed, scores of them. He looked at his watch. Ten minutes to eleven. No, it hadn't stopped. Up came Hans with a steaming mug of coffee and a great grin.

"Like?" he said. Hans wasted no words in gales.

"Like," said Yank, and poured the stuff down. It was strong.

At that moment there was a shout from Taffy, in the bows. He was pointing at something which the lads made out to be a great clod of craggy land, black and glowering.

"Wales?" said Hans.

"Yep." After all, it wasn't likely to be any other place.

"Oh-ho," said Hans.

At any rate it was where it ought to be, well clear on the ship's lee bow. Yank judged it to be the bulge of Llangelynin by Barmouth. Taffy couldn't help in its identification. He didn't know these waters. But he allowed that Yank was probably right. He ran down to see if Mr. Hughes was conscious to give his advice on the matter. But the Mate was still dead to the world.

Yank stood on. When the ketch got past this bulge and along past Towyn, she would be in a good position to go round and stand northwards again, on the other tack. He daren't let her go free at all, to help her speed. Some time later, a buoy suddenly loomed up in a slight clearing in the rain, perhaps half a mile away. It could not be the Bwch, for they were too far inshore of that—must be so. So it could only be the buoy which marked the entrance to the fairway off Aberdovey Bar. Then the breakers would soon be alee—were there now! The ship was making better speed than he had thought. She was fairly racing along. Aye, it was Aberdovey Outer all right! How maddening that they could not go in! He'd have a go at it, if only there was a bit of water on the bar.... But now it would be murder. To race through those thundering breakers, unable to see one channel-marking buoy from the next—and probably not able to see any at all—would be a nightmare at the best of times. Now, it would be certain death. If the sands of that dreadful bar once came up to smash at the ketch's keel, she was finished. She would be smashed to pieces in a matter of moments, and no one would live.

"Ready about!" Yank shouted. "We'll wear her around!"

They could hear the breaking of the seas thundering on the bar. Just at that moment the weather suddenly cleared, and all the bar showed up before them in its awful roaring majesty. Sail into that? No, no! It would be madness! It was frightening even to know that such a place existed. For a moment or two the visibility was excellent. They could see the little coastguard hut by the cemetery, and make out the refuge tower on the sands, and, beyond that, the flagstaff at the wharf. The coastguard would be able to see them, too, and know at least that the ship was all right—so far. What they could not know was the condition of Mr. Hughes, and that the boys were in complete charge of the ship.

Now the value of the drill they had gone through on the way to Abersoch—was it only the previous day?—became apparent, as the boys fought to their places for wearing round. They knew what to do. The ship must run off before the wind and then come up again with the wind on the other side, and the sails would have to go over at the proper time. That was the question. Could the gear stand the awful griping stresses which were inevitably involved? Yank knew it was a chance. But it was a chance that must be taken, and at once! But if she'd sailed across the Causeway, he told himself, she could do anything. After that, all risks were minor. He gave the teak and brassbound wheel an affectionate pat.

Tiny signalled that all was ready. Yank put the wheel

up to let the ship run off. Tiny paid out a little main sheet. The boom tackle was ready to take the strain as the boom swung, when the time came, so that it could not take charge and run amok.... How the ship seemed to race towards the breakers, as if her sole aim was to get among them and commit an instant suicide! There was a moment when she must run deliberately towards this gravest danger, before she could be brought up on the other tack. Yank kept his head. Hans the Icelander, Chum Jones, Tich Edwards, Tiny Donaldson, Mike, Taffy—all of them—well knew the danger. He looked at their set, tense faces. Already they looked like men, not boys.... The ship was coming round nicely. Even then, he admired the beauty with which she steered and handled.

"Now!" he shouted.

"Now!" shouted the boys. Tiny set up the other main backstay and his shipmate Edwards immediately slacked away alee. Hans had charge of the main sheet. Chum Jones looked to the boom tackle. Brum Shrivenham and little Senussian were looking after the mizzen (which didn't matter so much). Pete Cordoba, Don Wiggins, Curly Mathieson (who had been most dreadfully seasick) and Mike O'Leary hauled manfully on whatever the other boys told them to haul. The stays'l looked after itself. The ship rolled furiously, stumbled in her stride, came up to the wind again as if she had been struck a violent blow. For a moment she faltered—poor ship! she had been asked to take a lot that morning—and then, slowly at first and then bravely and without hesitation, she gathered way and thrashed along. To wind'ard! To wind'ard! The Aberdovey Outer buoy and all the land had disappeared and the thunder of the breakers was lost in the roaring of the wind.

So far, so good; but dear Lord, please bring us to St. Tudwal's Roads, Yank prayed as he bent once more over the bucking wheel.

9

Through Bardsey Sound

FROM Aberdovey Bar to St. Tudwal's Roads is about forty miles. Making some six knots, it would take the ship six or seven hours to reach the anchorage, but the wind was hauling free a little and her speed was bound to increase. Maybe she would make it in four and a half hours. She was all right now as far as the Bwch shoals and the Causeway were concerned, for she could weather them both.

The time then was about noon, and the weather, though still bad, seemed inclined to relent. They were abeam of the Bwch buoy less than forty minutes after wearing round. They passed near enough to read the name, and the big ketch was racing. Past the buoy, now that he was sure of his position, Yank allowed the ship to go on to the compass course and fall a little from the wind. It was easier for her and easier on her masts and sails, and gear. How she raced along! The sprays still clouded her, but they did not now drive over her so viciously nor clump themselves with such violence to the tops of her masts. She ran like a big thoroughbred and took every sea like a good old steeplechaser which, though tired and sorely tried, could still be relied upon to jump true and strong at every obstacle.

With the breather, Yank organised the boys again. Curly Mathieson tried to organise some food in the galley but could not stand the motion there, and the lack of air. Hans and Chum Jones hacked some fishermen's slices from five loaves of bread and passed them out with hunks of cheese. Many of the boys did not care to eat. They could keep going and they could work, but they had no interest in food.

From time to time they went down to have a close look at Mr. Hughes, but he showed no change. Yank was anxious to get the ship back to St. Tudwal's Roads in order to get a doctor for the old Mate. He saw the place again, in his mind's eye. It was a good place to make, so long as you could see it before you went in. But there were some fearful places nearby in which a ship could become embayed and hopelessly lost, if she mistook the headland. That was easy enough to do on such a day as this, for one Welsh headland, looming suddenly up in the rain, looked alarmingly like another. If he ran off too far and held a course too far easterly, there was a nasty chance of getting among the rocks off St. Tudwal's Island where the bell buoy clanged its warning, or—what was almost as bad—to fetch up once again down to leeward of the Roads and be driven into that horrible lee corner from which they had so recently escaped. Yank kept the ship up, thinking of that—anything was better than *that*. Unconsciously, almost, he kept the ship to wind'ard, always a little to the west'ard of her course. Better to be to windward than to leeward. He must trust to luck to see something.

Each boy in turn came to the wheel, for it was not quite so necessary to keep only the best there now. To steer under such conditions was a memorable experience. Some of the lads had the ship swinging violently at times, but sooner or later, they got the hang of it. Ten minutes at the wheel of the racing ship under those conditions was better than a month of other helmsmanship. They *had* to learn, and learn fast. It was incredible that they had been in the ship little more than 24 hours. Already most of them felt like Cape Horn veterans.

They raced towards the Causeway buoy, watching for it anxiously and listening, too, as the patent log streaming astern showed the ship had run about the distance.... Ah, there it was! At least a mile from where they thought it ought to be, away out on the port beam. But the chart showed there was plenty of water inside there for the *Warspite;* the buoy was placed well out from the western edge of the line of rocks. But Yank was shaken.

"This darned bay!" he muttered to Taffy. "A fellow'd have to be born here to know his way around! Now, I thought I was allowing plenty to get to wind'ard of that buoy."

"Plenty of people born around here get drowned here, too," said Taffy.

"Huh. You're cheerful. Well, I guess it'd be difficult

to be born around here and be cheerful too. Look out fine now for St. Tudwal's, Taff."

Taffy went into the bows. After a while, Hans climbed into the main rigging the better to keep lookout from there. The weather was thickening again and there was little sign of early improvement.

It was Hans who first made out the loom of the land, a great cliff towering right ahead, almost upon them! Taffy saw it the next second and came racing aft.

"Look out!" he shouted. "Look out! Look out for Hell's Mouth! Bring her up, Yank! We've missed the Roads!"

"Flatten in the sheets, lads!" shouted Yank, as he ran to the wheel to bring the ship up to the wind. They could see the broken creaming water roaring at the base of the great grey cliff, and hear it washing there. The ship, responding to her wheel with grace and speed as she always did, came up to the wind again. They flattened in the sheets until she was lying close-hauled again on the port tack, heading somewhere west.

"Hell's Mouth!" shouted Taffy. "If we get in there we won't come out again! Head westwards for Bardsey Sound. It's our only chance!"

"Huh," said Yank, "I dunno about Hell's Mouth, but my heart's in mine. I'm fed up with this Cardigan Bay!"

"Bardsey Sound'll bring us out of it. It's the strait between the Isle of Saints and the western end of Wales. I know the way. I'll get her through there for you."

"And where in all heck do we go then?"

"Ah, we can run for Nevin, then, and get her anchor

down at Porth Dinlleyn." He called it something that sounded like "Porth-thinthlane."

"Where?"

"Porth Dinlleyn. It's my home, you know. It's a grand little place, once you get in."

Yank glanced at him a moment, dubiously. He couldn't recall from his hurried examinations of the chart any point which qualified as a 'grand little place' anywhere along that whole wild coast. But the problem at the moment was to keep out of this place called Hell's Mouth.

"I'm all right steering west, meantime?" he asked.

"Aye. It will do. But keep her to wind'ard as well as you can. We'll have the tide with us through Bardsey and we'll run like a racehorse there."

"How wide's this Sound of yours, Taffy?"

"Ah, wide enough. About half a mile at the narrowest."

"And full of rocks, I guess."

"No, no. Bardsey Sound's clear enough itself. And the tide just rips through. If its against a ship she cannot go, for it brings up such a sea she'd never live in it."

Yank wondered about Bardsey Sound. It sounded a bit like the Pentland Firth to him, and, at the moment, they couldn't see either the high mainland of Wales nor Bardsey Island—the Isle of the Saints as Taffy had called it, for 20,000 saints of Wales were buried there. He had to take the thing on trust. At any rate, every yard the good ketch sailed was putting them further and further out of the dangerous lee corner of Tremadoc Bay. That, at least, was astern.

"When we saw that headland sudden like," said Taffy, "I couldn't be sure whether it was Tryn Cilan or the bluff at the western end of the Mouth of Hell. This is no place to take chances! Many a ship's done that. They've thought they'd seen Cilan and run in for the Roads, only to get in the breakers. Too late, then! So I shouted to you to bring her up and to keep to wind'ard.... Now I'm not sure how far it is to the island, but we'll see."

"I *hope* we'll see," said Yank. "And you'd better hope so too. And there isn't a deal of daylight left now."

He peered anxiously to windward. Taffy'd said that it was safe to approach Bardsey Island close-to, for the water was deep that side, and there weren't many rocks. But it was nerve-wracking to be standing yet once more towards a dangerous place with another so close and so threatening, right under their lee. Only let's get through this place Bardsey Sound, Yank hoped—and then—well, at any rate the ship would have a bit of sea room. Next stop Ireland, or perhaps this place Nevin.

Meanwhile the ketch boiled along in a flurry of spray and spume and foam, and again the thick seas clouded over her. Once for a few moments she was in a boiling of the waters almost as bad as the breakers on the Causeway, and the sea leapt and fumed all round her as if it had quite gone mad and was no longer capable even of running true. At the same time it was making an awful sound, crying and sighing. It was an eerie experience, and frightening.

"The Devil's Tail!" shouted Taffy. "We're doing all right."

"All right, you call it! You can have your Devil's Tail!"

"But I know where we are, now. There's only one place like that near abouts here. Its foul ground, spoiling the water."

"Foul's the name for it!"

"Well now, we're making a good course for Bardsey Sound. That's something."

Yank agreed whole-heartedly with that last remark, and looked round anxiously to see what next the furious waters of Cardigan Bay might throw in the ship's path. Why, the whole place ought not to be called a bay at all. It was nothing but a torment of the waters, a series of holes in the frightful water into which good ships could fall. He thought he understood, now, why the ancient navigators often drew fierce dragons on their charts, waiting with their mouths open to bite down big ships. It looked as if they could literally happen, right there in Cardigan Bay! Maybe the artists had been Portmadoc men, who habitually had to contend with this kind of thing.

"Wind's gone flukey now," said Tiny, who was standing close by Yank. "I expect we must be getting in the lee of Bardsey Island. Sea's gone down a bit too—or it would if the foul bottom and the racing tide would let it."

"Aye, it's gone down. It won't be so bad there," Taffy chimed in. "You fellows are getting the wrong idea entirely of this lovely cruising ground."

"Cruising ground my blooming eye!" shouted Chum Jones derisively. "Who wants to cruise around a place called Hell's Mouth, with the Devil's Tail to ride him!"

"Ah, but its lovely in the summer. Hundreds of yachts come cruising here, I'll have you know."

"Not with me in any of 'em," shouted Chum Jones.

"Nor blooming-well me either!" said Brum, with a grim look on his face.

"When's the blooming summer, may I ask?" chimed in young Don Wiggins, his teeth chattering with the cold. The lad was wet right through and had not been able to eat anything.

"Some years we have good summers," said Taffy proudly.

"What? Some *years*, did you say!" said Yank, horrified. "Do you mean you can go for years without a real summer here at all?"

"Ah, there's always many days that's champion fine," Taffy defended his native climate. "But some years is better than others. Now look at our Icelander there. He thinks this *is* good weather. The trouble with you fellows is you've been spoiled. Now there's a chap that knows what bad weather really is."

Taffy looked at Hans with admiration. The Iceland lad grinned.

"Coffee?" he asked, hopefully.

"Coffee, yes!" they all shouted. "You make it?"

"Oh-oh," said Hans, and dived for the companion as the ship made a wild swipe at the sea and scooped her jibboom into green water. The loom of the high land on their starboard beam by this time was clearly to be seen, and now the ship was racing by a pinnacle of rock with the tide fairly boiling past it. The water was rushing at the weather side of the rock as if it was quite insane with anger that the rock should be there at all, and was ferociously determined to smash it down. Poor Wales, with all this stormy water for ever roaring at her! Yank watched the onrush of the sea. He shivered, for the moment. It would be an awful sea to be spilled into. Men who fished round here must be sailors indeed, like those old Portmadoc boys and the men of all that wild peninsula. No wonder they were seamen! And thank heavens the tide was with the *Warspite* now. The old ketch must be making better than fourteen knots over the ground, for the tide was racing five.

"Like a racehorse, Yank, isn't she?" said Tiny. "It's good to be here. I mean, I don't know where we're going or where we'll fetch up. But I wouldn't be anywhere else —not for anything."

"You know, Tiny, that's just the way I feel. Funny, isn't it? With the rain streaming down my neck and the ship trying to turn somersaults, and the sea racing up astern trying to swamp us there and smash us down. Yet I wouldn't be anywhere else, not for anything!"

"Nor me either. I ought to be at classes aboard the *Conway* now, if it wasn't for this course. Good old course!"

"I wouldn't mind now being in Oxford," said young Don Wiggins. "I don't see this is so wonderful. Give me my feet on dry land! They're going to stay there, once I get 'em that way again."

"Ah, you haven't got the right spirit," said Tiny. "You'd be better with a feed inside you."

"If I could only keep it down!"

"You'll get used to this, Don."

"Danged if I wants to stay that long."

They all grinned at this. Meanwhile the ship must have been racing through the sound, with Bardsey Island, all unseen, to wind'ard. Visibility was perhaps quarter of a mile, and they were very close to the coast of Wales. Now they raced from rock to rock with the breaking water on the cliff-bases seemingly only a few yards away.

"It's all steep-to—safe enough. Keep her as she goes, Yank," said Taffy. "I see the wind outside isn't so bad, either, if we can judge by the sea."

They could see the open waters of the Irish Sea now, leaping beyond the Sound. The chart was open on the seat inside the deckhouse where it could be consulted quickly. Taffy knew the coast without a chart.

"Braich-y-Pwll!" he shouted, suddenly, pointing to a grim high bluff towering in the murk almost above them. "It's the end of the Sound. You can keep close to yon and let her fall off as soon's she's by, and run for Nevin!"

The big ketch came storming by the cliff at what looked like twenty knots and was probably all of fifteen, for she was feeling the gale again beyond the brief shelter of Bardsey. She put her shoulder down and tore along in a welter of foam, and, as she rounded the point and fell off before the wind to race towards Nevin, she strained and leapt as if she might almost take off and become a jet-propelled airplane at any moment. She was carrying too much sail. Yank knew that. But the anchorage at Porth Dinlleyn was still fifteen miles away, and he knew they must make it before dark. Taffy said the ship could keep close inshore, picking up the high land from time to time. Most dangers, he said, were very close to the beach. He knew them all.

"I'm looking forward to a good meal when that anchor's down," he said. "She'll lie there snug's a bug in a rug. You see!"

It was difficult for the boys to believe that any ship could lie snug anywhere along that grim and mountainous coast. Very dubious about it, Yank closely examined the chart for the twentieth time. Quite close in by the beach at Port Dinlleyn it was true there might be good anchorage for very small vessels. But the ketch drew over eleven feet of water, and she could not get into the best places. Besides, the bay looked horribly open to him. It was all right while the wind was south of west, but if the wind worked round to anything north of west—as inevitably it must—then they would have to get out, and get out fast, for they would be on a terrible lee shore.

At a few minutes before six he slipped below to have a look again at Mr. Hughes, who seemed to be sleeping heavily, and to hear the B.B.C.'s weather forecast. "Before the weather forecast, there are gale warnings to shipping in the Irish Sea..." and a dozen other places, the forecast began as soon as he turned the radio on. It went on to speak of a fresh westerly gale in the Irish Sea and Lundy, which would be severe at times but would veer slowly to the north-west. Veer slowly to the northwest! Then Porth-Dinlleyn would be impossible.

Yank went up on deck and called a council of war.

"This place Porth-what's-its name won't do," he said. "The wind's going around to N.W. soon."

"Who says that, Yank?" asked Taffy.

"The B.B.C."

"Ah, the blessed B.B.C.! They're always slandering our weather!"

"Not without cause," said Tiny. "Doesn't the wind always finish up in that quarter though, Taffy?"

"Aye, often it does. But it takes time to veer around. Maybe we could get the night in."

"Maybe! Maybe won't do." Yank shook his head.

"There's a good lifeboat at Porth-Dinlleyn," said Taffy.

"Lifeboat? We won't be needing that, thank you," Yank was vehement. "But Tiny, what about making for these straits between this island here—I see Anglesey's the name—and the mainland? Your *Conway's* there, isn't she? Is it any use for shelter?"

"The *Conway's* far up Menai Straits," said Tiny. "I've never been down at this Caernarvon Bay end. But I know there's a very bad bar across there. I should think it would be hopeless in this sort of weather. It would be night, too, you remember, by the time we get there."

"Its quite hopeless to get in there without a pilot, and he'd not come out in this gale," said Taffy. "He couldn't. No, don't go there, Yank. We'd get jammed on a lee shore again, up there."

"What a place! You'd think it was designed just to harass ships. Well, what do you suggest? How about further north, now? There's this place around the corner—Holyhead. I've heard of that. It's a shelter port, isn't it, with long breakwaters?"

"Aye, its a fine place. We could make for there. But there are bad rocks round Holy Island.... Maybe its the best we can do," Taffy agreed gloomily, loth to give up the idea of going to his beloved Nevin.

"Do you agree, Tiny? Shall we try for Holyhead?"

"Yes, Yank. It's a good place. We'd certainly be all right if we once get in there."

"Iceland, you have a look at the chart. We're figuring on making for this place here, this Holyhead. Around the corner there by the North Stack. What do you think of it?"

Yank and all the lads had learned to respect the Icelander's sea sense, that long wild day. But it seemed that the idea of getting shelter hadn't occurred to the flaxen-haired lad. He had thought they were merely having a good sail. He looked from Yank to Tiny and from Tich Edwards to Chum Jones, who were also in the council.

"Holyhead?" he asked, dubiously.

"Yes, that place there." Yank pointed with a big wet finger.

"What for?"

"Shelter. Get the anchor down. Fix up the Mate. Get a doctor."

"Oh, fix the Mate? Okay. Let's go."

So it was decided. Holyhead it was. Yank went out on deck and brought the ship to the wind again, to lie the new course from the Nevin Peninsula over towards the western end of Holy Island.

With luck, she might make it by midnight, and, at any rate, now she had sea room. He was not going to sail into any more diabolical bays.

10

Off the Windy Stack

"WE'LL set up a proper routine," Yank was saying, "and we'll keep to the watches as they were fixed when we came aboard, except we'll make four watches of it for the night, in case we're out all night. We'll be three in each watch. I'll take one, Tiny another, Edwards the third, and Iceland here the other one. I'll have Taffy and Chum Jones in my watch. Is that okay, chaps?"

"It's all right with us," said Taffy and the Chum.

"Who'd you like with you, Tiny?"

"I'll have Mike and Brum."

"What about you, Hans?"

"Okay," said the Icelander, nodding towards little Nicky Senussian and Pete Cordoba.

This left Curly Mathieson and Don Wiggins for Tich Edwards' watch. All being well, they would not be called on, for the arrangement was that each watch would last three hours.

"One fellow in each watch looks after the Mate," said Yank. "That leaves one for lookout and one for the wheel. Change about every hour. Now, Taffy, you'd better have a look at Mr. Hughes. We've been a bit neglectful of him and I'm sorry about it, but we've all been pretty fully occupied with the ship. Maybe if you speak Welsh to him nicely he'll come around."

"And the chap looking after the Mate makes some coffee, too. Or maybe tea. And toast," put in Tiny.

"Tea?" glared the Icelander, horrified. He regarded tea as a most unmaritime beverage, but he was howled down.

When nightfall came, the ketch was reaching towards the South Stack, intending to round that obstruction with a good offing, in wild weather. But there was a hope of better conditions before too long. Now and again, a star peeped out in a passing clearing, and when it was well dark, they could make out the loom of some powerful lights. Very few of the boys had gone below. Those not actually on watch were huddled in their oilskins in the lee of the deckhouse or in a corner of the counter abaft the wheel, by a grating. It was driest there. It was pretty wet everywhere.

Yank's watch was from six to nine p.m., then Tiny until midnight, then Tich Edwards to 3 a.m., and Hans the Icelander from 3 to 6. At nine o'clock the ketch was still doing quite well, under the same short canvas she had been carrying most of the day—close-reefed main and mizzen and a reefed fore stays'l. The sails loomed up black in the thick night and the howling of the strong wind in the rigging was mournful and sad. But the B.B.C. nine o'clock news spoke of a possible moderation in the morning, though it was still full of gale warnings.

Yank looked in at Mr. Hughes. He was still the same,

chocked in his bunk in a deep sleep, or perhaps he was still unconscious. Taffy had made him as comfortable as possible, and the little cabin which the Mate shared with the engineer was tolerably warm. Yank listened to the sea swishing by so close outside, just beyond the planks.

Then he had a good look at the chart again. That place Holyhead looked good. It ought to be simple enough, to sail in there. There was a book of sailing directions aboard, for the whole of the United Kingdom coasts. He looked up Holyhead. Those infernal Sailing Directions books always mentioned every possible danger and difficulty—they had to, of course—and the pages of this volume made Holyhead seem completely impossible, an unreachable haven hemmed in by a labyrinth of unsufferable dangers. Huh! Yank grunted and shut the book. Blast all Sailing Directions! The place was well enough lit. He'd cope with it when the time came. He'd a good picture of the entrance in his mind, and figured out what he would do.

He was still turning over in his mind the best way to bring a big ketch under sail into the Roads of Holyhead as he stretched out on the deckhouse settee, without taking off a stitch—not even his sou'wester— and prepared himself for an hour or two's rest. Good old Tiny had the deck now. If anything happened, Tiny would call him and they would see what they could do. Let me see now, he thought, this place Holyhead...he'd keep everything set until he was well inside...must keep good way! There'd be a set across the entrance between the breakwaters, and it would be folly to get the ship smashed up on a stone wall when she had been through so much. The wind's howl was slightly muffled, in there in the deckhouse with the doors closed. Now and again a cloud of heavy spray hit the weather side with a clump, and arms of water like little rivers ran down everywhere.... Gosh! but he was tired. He couldn't remember ever having felt so tired in his life before, not even on the Bermuda race.

It seemed about five minutes later, actually it was over two hours, when he was awakened by a wild thrashing of canvas and thundering like heavy gunfire. Good lord, what now?

"Mains'l gone!" shouted Tiny, thrusting a wet head inside the deckhouse for an instant. "I'm getting all hands up!"

Yank dashed out. Above his head the great gaff was flailing and banging and enormous wraiths of blown-out canvas were twisting and thundering. The main deck was lit brilliantly every few seconds by the powerful beam of a revolving light standing upon some rocks off the starboard bow. This was the South Stack, the way to Holyhead. But there could be no Holyhead now! The mains'l had to come down. The wind had eased somewhat—and thank heaven for that—but with only the mizzen and the stays'l set, she couldn't fool around by night trying to run between the breakwaters at Holyhead. Or at any other strange haven.

First that mains'l must come down. Yank shouted to the lad at the wheel—it was Mike—to keep well off the light.

"Steer for Ireland, Mike!" he yelled when he saw in the binnacle's light who it was. Although the sail had gone only a moment or so, Tiny already had things as well under control as they could be. The boom was hauled midships, and a group of boys was lowering away on the peak and throat halliards while others were hauling down on the vang, the line which kept the gaff in order, or was supposed to do so. But no vang could check the gaff when half the blown-out mains'l was clinging to it and the whole peak of the sail was trying to twist the gaff from its jaws altogether, quite out of control. The gaff would not come down. The vang, unable to stand the strain, carried away. At that moment, the great light from the lighthouse showed a boy—two boys—struggling up the rigging to windward. The ship was rolling violently without the mainsail to steady her, though she was still going through the water quite well. Up, up the two figures climbed, now swung out above the sea, now rolled inboard above the decks. Their oilskins gleamed in the lighthouse beams as they fought their way up, step by step. Often they could only cling to the shrouds for their lives while the sea boiled below them and the ship lurched as if she were intoxicated, or trying deliberately to shake them down. But slowly, steadily, they climbed. They were making for the jaws of the gaff, to ride the gaff down, hoping that their weight would turn the scales and force the gaff to descend. At the same time, they could work the halliards to help the stiff wire and sodden hemp through the blocks. Good idea! Now they were up. They'd reached the gaff. Yank saw one figure stand on the very jaws. The other, climbing slowly past him, reached out, jumped for the gaff, and sat the gaff like a broncho-buster on a wild mustang. Riding it down, by thunder! He'd need to ride well!

Yank took a second to get a quick bearing on the light. She mustn't be set on that, and already she was almighty close.

He jumped to the main saloon skylight, fisting the wet canvas with half a dozen lads, getting the canvas in—such as was left of it—helping to fight the gaff down from the jaws outwards. It was coming now, but coming with horrible slowness. But still, descending. A great area of the sail blew out with a tremendous burst and flung itself to leeward, flying off through the shrieking air as if its first stop would be the North Pole. Other cloths parted, and the air to leeward became a snarl of flying, twisting, wind-maddened canvas. Poor sail! But it came in the better now that there was so much the less of it. The gaff-end was still flailing like a crane-arm in an earthquake. But it was coming. The lads tried to lassoo it from the deck. The figure astride the gaff was slowly working his way out. He caught the lassoo, secured the end—under control! The gaff came down quickly now, and the remains of the sail were roughly secured. The lads lashed the gaff to the boom in a fashion—not very seamanlike, perhaps. But it would do. Neither gaff nor boom could cause any damage now.

Yank saw it was Tiny who'd been riding the jaws of the gaff, and the Icelander who'd been further out.

J.M.D.C.

"Nice work, Tiny!" he said, and grinned in the light-beams at the Icelander. Hans was sniffing where the galley funnel had been, probably hoping for some sign of coffee.

"Well, there goes our hopes of Holyhead," Tiny said. "It seems like the old ship *wants* to keep the sea, and give us a good run for our money. How about Ireland, Yank? Isn't that place Kingstown or Dun Laoghaire or whatever it is more or less abeam of here? And Dublin? Let's ask Mike."

"Mike now, do you know the way into Dublin, or Dun Laoghaire?" asked Yank, taking a quick look across the compass at the South Stack Light. She was making on that, anyway. Probably the tide must still be with her.

"I could take you all there in a bus, or on a train now," said Mike, who had a grip of the wheel as if it were the steering-wheel of a recalcitrant steam-roller.

The boys laughed. Mike scratched his head.

"That isn't much use!" snorted Tiny. "This isn't a bus, you know, or a train!"

"It's awful wild water off those parts I know, too," said Mike. "There's banks and shoals all along the coast from Dublin Bay down. There's the Kish and the Codling light-ships there, now, to give warning. Maybe we *could* get in."

"And maybe we could not," said Yank. "Ah well, we'll keep this easy canvas on her for the night now and see where we get in the morning. We'll get a good offing from this clump of bad-tempered rocks around here and run along northwards through the Irish Sea. Then when that nor'westerly comes, the broadcast spoke about, we can turn around and run back again."

"There's Liverpool," said Tiny. "And there's the Isle of Man."

"We'll find somewhere. It'll clear sooner or later. Why it's clearing all the time right now," said Yank. "You go below now, Tiny. It's well past midnight. We'll give Edwards his watch and he can keep her running up in the middle of the Irish Sea. Nothing much can happen to her there."

Tich Edwards took over the watch, going to the wheel. Curly Mathieson went down to look after Mr. Hughes, and young Wiggins went to the lookout. A last bearing showed Yank that the ship was perfectly all right, for the time being. She was not being set towards the land, and, with the small canvas she was carrying, she could scarcely come to much harm. He went below to have a look at the chart, and read up on Liverpool and the Isle of Man. But the Sailing Directions were horribly pessimistic on both subjects. Liverpool, it seemed, lay on the banks of a dreadful river which had to be kept in check with revements on which sailing ships could come to fearful grief, and the surrounding dangers were infinite and varied. As for the Isle of Man, it seemed a good idea to give the whole place as wide a berth as possible. Oh, for the deep blue sea!

The ship ran on quietly through the night. She had not so much speed now, and parts of the main deck were almost dry by the dawn. The dawn came cheerless enough, and grey, with a threat of fog. There was no land in sight, nothing but the grey cold sea and the black ketch reeling on her way. They saw the lights of big ships often enough in the night, once or twice, indeed, too close for comfort. But daylight brought nothing.

At six, Hans the Icelander roused up all hands with a piping pot of coffee and a great jug of tea. It turned out that he had boiled the water and the tea leaves together throughout his watch, but the intention was good, and all who had leather stomachs gulped the stuff down. He'd found some mackerel lines in a deck locker, too, and these trailed astern, with the lads of his watch taking turns to look after them. Every few moments, a big mackerel struck at one or other of the lines and was promptly hauled in and put in a bucket. There must have been twenty or thirty already. The Icelander showed the boys how to split them easily, and remove the bones. Then he spread the split fish on the top of the carley float to dry.

"Good for breakfast!" he said. "Okay!"

"Okay," said Yank. "You fry 'em, Iceland."

This the Icelander did by the simple means of rolling the fish in dry oatmeal and then putting the lot of them into a big deep dish with a little fat, which he put into the oven. Meanwhile the other lads, under Yank's and Tiny's direction, removed the skylight covers to let some air circulate down below, and tidied up generally. The mains'l was an awful mess, but the decks were all right and there was nothing adrift aloft. The sail had gone when a cloth was chafed through, weakening the whole. Down below there was some sight pandemonium where things had spilled out of the boys' gear, and so on. But she was not too bad. It was not the first time the ketch had been in a blow, and things down below had been well secured.

A grand meal of fried mackerel and bread with more of what the Icelander called tea gave the day a bully start. Now there was a touch of pale sun, though the visibility was still very poor.

"What do you say, we shift the mains'l and bend the mizzen there?" said Yank. "I've looked all through the ship and there certainly isn't a spare main aboard. I've tried the Mate, too, but he's still out. I guess there isn't room to carry a spare big sail like that, and fit a dozen boys in too."

"Her other mains'ls are in the locker on the wharf at Aberdovey," said Tiny. "Yes, good idea, Yank. We'll get on with it right away. She can wander along under the stays'l with the reef shaken out meantime. She won't come to any harm."

The lads got to work at once, leaving one at the wheel and one standing by down below in case Mr. Hughes revived. Once or twice the Mate had stirred uneasily, but as yet he showed no signs of returning to consciousness.

Shifting the blown-out sail was not much of a job, and the lads bundled it down below without ceremony. It could wait until the ship was back at Aberdovey. Getting the mizzen changed was a bit more work. But it progressed steadily. The B.B.C. weather forecasts still spoke of gale warnings and gales and more vile weather, though the Irish Sea was not being specifically singled out for further horrors at the moment.

"Before the weather forecast, there are warnings of gales in sea areas..." and so forth and so on, every time.

"As soon as that guy says 'Before,' I fear the worst," said Yank. "Taffy and his cruising ground."

Taffy looked hurt.

"Where are we off to now, Yank?" asked Mike. "How about Dublin Bay?"

"It's me for the open water while the visibility's as bad as this. We're past Dublin already," Yank replied. "Say, do any of you guys know any place on the Isle of Men?"

"Isle of Man you mean," said Tiny. "I've never been there. Have you, Edwards?"

"No, Tiny." A chorus of noes from the others clinched that. Nobody knew the way into Douglas or anywhere else on the Isle of Man.

"All we've got to do is thread a way past. Let's go the Irish side," Yank concluded. "If so be it does clear up, maybe we can have a crack at getting in some place. And what about that nor'west wind the broadcasters promised us? It looks mighty like S.W. to me."

Indeed the wind was sticking at S.W., though each forecast in turn throughout the day spoke of coming north-west winds in the Irish Sea. Nor did the visibility improve. While the ship was wandering slowly along under her stays'l only, a whole line of little ships meandered across her bow, all bound directly westwards.

"Tide time in the Mersey," said Tiny. "That's the coasters going to Ireland."

J.M.D.C.

There were small steamers with enormous green funnels, curious old-timers with their engines aft and thin high smoke-stacks looking like upended cigarettes and, as far as anyone could see, not a soul on deck. Little steamer after little steamer seemed to be wandering along on her own, finding her own way to Ireland without the aid of any human beings. There was no one in sight to hail.

"Well, they've given us a check on where we are, anyway," Yank remarked, appreciatively.

"Let's follow 'em now," said Mike, with brilliant inspiration.

"At this speed, Mike lad? How the dickens can we? Look boy, the half of 'em are lost in the mist again already. If we'd the gale now, we could do it all right, and sail around 'em."

There was obviously nothing to do but wander on. They set the mizzen as a mainsail, and the ketch sailed northwards very pleasantly. At any rate for the time being, she was coming to no harm.

The day passed with no change. Still Mr. Hughes lay in his bunk below, dead to the world.

11

The North Atlantic

"I GUESS we might as well have a crack at sailing right around Ireland," said Yank gloomily, as the boys listened to the early morning weather forecast down in the saloon. It spoke of fresh to strong southerly in the Irish Sea, increasing later to gale force, severe at times and veering to south-west. "What happened to that nor'wester they promised us?"

"Guess it petered out," said Tiny. "They often do, you know. But I like that idea of yours, Yank. Let's have a go! Right around Ireland! I've always wanted to do that."

"Well, it looks like we'll get back to Aberdovey as quick that way as any other. How far is it now?"

The charts were open on the table, and the lads pored over them with dividers and parallel rules. Tiny measured off the approximate distance.

"I make it to be about 700 sailing miles from about where we are now, in the North Channel, right around and back to Aberdovey. That's allowing for giving the land a good offing the whole way. It might take us a week or more."

"Or a fortnight! Well, we haven't much choice now than to continue to run before the wind and thread the ship up here through this place, the North Channel." Yank studied the chart. "Let's see now. That's Scotland. Darn it, I wanted to see that place too. This side's Ireland. We've got to run through and out here south of this place Islay. Then we're in the North Atlantic. We give Ireland a berth, bowl on down the west side, whizz around the corner by Fastnet here, and then wham-ho! for Aberdovey!"

"Why do you think we can bowl along southwards west of Ireland when we can only scud to the nor'ard here, Yank?"

It was Taffy who asked the question.

"It's a hope, Taff. But look, this is the way I figure it. At any rate we've got these B.B.C. weather forecasts to give us the weather outlook. Seems to me like the wind almost always starts in the south and sou'west around these parts, and then maybe or not it blows like the devil. Then it hauls west and around to nor'west, and blows itself out from there. The way I figure it, we've had a bellyful of south and sou'west now, and we must be due for nor'-west some time. I'll gamble on running her every mile we can get out of this southerly and then, about the time we're making west of Ireland, it'll be nor'west, and we'll scud before that."

"What, sail all round all Ireland without ever once going in? Past all that lovely island!" This was from Mike, of course.

"'Fraid so, Mike. But we might have to go in somewhere, of course. There's another thing, chaps. Mr. Hughes will be better one of these days. There's colour back in his face now and he's breathing better. He'll help us."

"Help us? I'll say! It'll be a mighty astonished Mr. Hughes that finds himself to the west'ard of Ireland. I'll bet!"

"Then we'll be about due for a sou'westerly blow again about the time we get off the Fastnet," Yank mused on, as much to himself as to the others. "Then, too, we'd have Queenstown to run for, and Waterford, and just around the corner into Rosslare, and all those places. We'd have sea-room, too. Danged if I want to go sailing a ship any more around these crowded, bad-tempered waters here! Did you see that big tanker brush past us around midnight? Fairly gave me a shave, he did! He whizzed within three inches of the old ship's side."

"And he wasn't the only one," said Tiny. "In my watch I got mixed up with a bunch of trawlers out of Fleetwood or somewhere. The whole place was buzzing with sirens and rushing ships. And some fast railway ferry had us rolling in her bow wave *and* her wake. I reckon we must've crossed the tracks of all the shipping bound for Belfast and up-channel for the Clyde, all the blooming night. It was a game!"

"Oh-oh!" said the Icelander, with a grin. "Plenty ships, plenty hurry! No good."

"Well, it might be a game," Yank concluded, "but it's a game I reckon I've had enough of. Okay! Now we've got to dodge this Mull of Kintyre and this Rathlin Island, and we still can't see a thing. Once I get out of all that

Irish Sea I'm not going back in there again – not ever."

"You know," said Chum Jones, "I suppose we could go into some place in Scotland, when it clears. And then the captain could come back and take her over."

"When it clears, did you say? That's the catch, Chum! *When* will it clear? Meantime we'd be past all Scotland and next stop Iceland! There's a lot of mouldy islands to pile up on around that Scots coast too. Besides here we are with a ship. It's a situation we aren't likely to find ourselves in again, or any other bunch of boys either. We won't give up that easy!"

"It wasn't giving up," said Chum Jones. "It was the navigation I was thinking of. Who can navigate?"

"We won't have to. We'll see something when it's clear. There's a sextant aboard and a nautical almanac. I can get a noon sight, come to that, and fix the latitude. That and the log'll do us. You chaps are good at chartwork – good enough, anyway. Come on now, around old Ireland!"

The project fired the boys' imaginations. A quick look in the coal bunker showed plenty of anthracite to keep the patent stove going for a fortnight, and a sounding in the freshwater tanks showed water enough. As for food, the mackerel were leaping for the hooks, and there were still all the supplies they had flung aboard off the Bar, and the ship's reserves as well. This consisted mainly of bully beef and biscuits, plenty of marmalade, and the makings of soup. Curly Mathieson was appointed permanent cook and steward to conserve supplies and dish out the food, and he said there should be little difficulty. There was even plenty of condensed milk for the coffee and tea, though some of the boys voted for eating up all the condensed milk at once in case they got seasick again if the weather worsened. This idea had something to commend it, but it was howled down.

On deck all was going well. True, the mizzen looked a trifle odd and very small, on the big mainmast, and there was nothing set at all on the mizzen mast. The stays'l and the big jib were set to help, and the patent log showed the ship to be doing at least five knots. It was still thick, and the foghorn was going up in the bows. Two lads were on lookout there, and the watch system was carried on through the day. The wind was slowly freshening again but the ship was under the lee of the land and there was no excessive motion. If only it would clear, the conditions would be quite enjoyable. Down below, Mr. Hughes appeared to be sleeping a little more comfortably. Both sides of his skylight were open to bring in good fresh air. Taffy and Chum Jones had bathed the old Mate's head again. They pronounced it much better. Mr. Hughes stirred once or twice while they tended him.

"He won't be long now," said Taffy.

"And a good job too," Chum Jones was worried. "I'm not over-trusting of these Yankee navigators and *Conway* chartwork!"

"Well, you can check it yourself, can't you now?"

Chum Jones piped down.

They heard the sirens of big ships more frequently than they wanted to, and once the great white bow wave of some liner, slowed down to twenty knots, came frightfully close.

"Thank the Lord for radar," Yank confided to Tiny. "I suppose most of these big ships do have radar, these days?"

"Aye, most of them. All liners have, at any rate. So they ought not to run into us."

"Pity we can't speak to one and send a message back to the school. They might be worried about us."

"'Might,' did you say? It's a strong 'might,' Yank! Our people will be worried, too. There's been no possible report of the ship since we showed her off the Dovey Bar."

"Well, we'll drive her along. We ought to see some fishermen, off Ireland anyway, when it clears. They've got two-way radio telephones these days, and they can send in a report. We won't say anything about Mr. Hughes," Yank continued. "Or they would be worried."

"We'd better listen to the B.B.C. news to see if there's anything about the ship," said Tiny. "So far we've only been listening to the weather."

Sure enough, the news at one o'clock mentioned the ship.

"No news has been received from the training ketch *Warspite* believed to be somewhere in the Irish Sea, since the vessel was blown away from Cardigan Bay several days ago," the announcer said. "The vessel is carrying twelve boys from the Outward Bound Sea School. No anxiety is felt as the Chief Officer, a man of considerable experience in sailing-ships, is aboard, but all shipping is requested to keep a lookout for the ketch."

"He'd be a bit more anxious if he could see his Chief Officer now," said young Edwards. "Chief Officer! I like that!"

"It does sound a phoney name for a good old Mate, aboard here. But they mean well. And it's a danged good thing they don't know what's happened to Mr. Hughes, too," said Yank.

There was nothing the boys could do to make the whereabouts of the ship known, except do their best to sail her back again. And right around Ireland! It might be a business. Still, as Yank and Tiny and the older lads agreed, there was nothing like being bold.

So the ketch sailed merrily on, gradually increasing speed, and Mr. Hughes was slowly mending, and the routine of the sea life settled over them all surprisingly well. Yank conducted the ship in style, with the proper bells and reports from helmsman and lookout and all that, as in a big sailing-ship, and he and Tiny and Tich Edwards and Hans walked the weather side of the little poop in turn. He was keeping as good a plot on the chart as he could, and the log readings were faithfully recorded in the rough deck-book, every hour. The boy at the wheel always smartly repeated the course, and the lad relieved repeated the course, too, as he went for'ard. The lookout came aft to report his relief. The decks were kept clear, the gear was seen to, the galley was spotless, the smell of damp was driven out of the quarters (except where the big wet heap of the blown-out mains'l lay), and Mr. Hughes could not have been better cared for if he'd had half-a-dozen state registered nurses looking after him.

"I dunno," Yank mused. "Danged if I wouldn't like to be making for St. John's. A feller could easily take to this life, Tiny."

"Newfoundland or New Brunswick?" asked Tiny, with a grin.

"Oh, you mean which St. John's? Newfoundland, Tiny. T'other is plain St. John. Besides, Newfoundland's nearer. I feel like that guy Cabot, or Cabotti, or whatever his name was. You know, the Italian guy who sailed across to Newfoundland from the west of England, when he heard about the Portuguese fishing there."

"I'd sooner be Captain Cook," said Tiny.

"Well, he spent plenty of time in Newfoundland too. And I guess he passed this way more than once. He had a humdinging little schooner in the Newfoundland survey for years."

"Why, Yank, you know more about him than I do. I always thought he just discovered Australia, and was murdered by the savages in Hawaii."

"Old Cook's always been one of my heroes. I've always studied those great sailors," said Yank, staring over the sea and striking a pose unconsciously rather like Christopher Columbus himself. "You know, I get bothered that there isn't any more discovering to do. Just imagine it now. You can feel a bit like Cook here. Imagine there wasn't any Australia on the maps yet, or New Zealand, or Hawaii, or New Caledonia, or the dozen other places he found! We'd have somewhere to go then, all right!"

"We wouldn't have any B.B.C. telling us the weather, though. Or liners keeping out of our way because they'd picked us up on their radar screens. We're lucky to be able to sail round Ireland, without half the destroyers in the fleet looking for us and a couple of salvage tugs racing out of Londonderry. Good job they don't know about Mr. Hughes!"

"Yeah, I guess we're lucky, at that. Come along, good breeze, bowl us along! And turn nicely to northwest or north some place by the corner, please."

"We'll be blessed lucky if it does that.... You know, I believe it is clearing a bit, though."

Indeed it was. The bad visibility was rolling back off the sea like a cloud slipping from a mountain-top, and the sunlight was streaming down as if anxious to make amends for its consistent absence earlier. It groped its way towards the ketch and suddenly found her, flooding the wet teak decks with glorious warmth and touching the sails to a spotless white. The boy on the lookout looked back and grinned, and the lad at the wheel grinned at him. The boys below came tumbling up the companion for'ard to bask in the sun. This was the life!

But the improved visibility disclosed the vessel sailing across a blue and empty sea. There was no sign of Ireland or Scotland, and there were no ships, or trawlers, or anything whatever to be seen.

"Steer W.S.W.," Yank called to the helmsman. "We'll pick up Inistrahull or Malin Head. Anyway, we must be out of the North Channel and clear of Scotland. Let her go!"

12

The Weather Makes Amends

"WE'RE darn lucky, that's what I say—here's the very wind we ordered, right where we wanted it! If you fellows think that sort of thing happens often in the North Atlantic, you've got another think coming. That's all that I can say!"

The speaker was Chum Jones.

"My father's been sailing the Western Ocean all his life and he hasn't a good word to say for it," put in Tich Edwards. "Maybe the sea gods think we had enough bad weather on the other side of Ireland."

"Whoever we've got to thank for it, I must say I'm mighty grateful, for one," chipped young Don Wiggins. "I'll have something to tell 'em when I gets backs to Leafield, now! I feel like Christopher Columbus."

"Senor Columbus was not sick like you, Donald," said Pete.

"I'm better now, Pete. I've been all right these last couple of days."

The ketch was slipping along before a lovely breeze out of the north-north-west, absolutely made to order. Away on her port beam the boys could see the blue haze of Ireland, somewhere about the Bloody Foreland. At least, Yank said it was *probably* some place in that area. He'd had a few shots at working up a position line by some patent method he said he had learned on the Bermuda race, but though the two *Conways* and Chum Jones helped him the whole morning and they took no end of observations, somehow that position line would persist in passing through either Cape Farewell, or the Chicago stock yards. Considering they were using an old alarm clock for a chronometer and none of them had much experience with the sextant, perhaps the line off Cape Farewell was not so bad.

Yank did get a good noon sight. Working that out was easy enough. He explained that all he had to do was to measure the altitude of the sun right at noon—and you could watch it climb in the sextant, and note when its climbing ceased and that was obviously noon—and then the Nautical Almanac told him the latitude where the sun was overhead. So the sun's altitude at the ship could be converted, by a simple calculation, into an indication—an accurate indication—of how far she was from the place where the sun was overhead. Hence the latitude was a simple matter of subtraction.

"Easy," said Yank.

"I don't get it," said Mike, and six or eight other boys echoed the sentiment.

"Anyway the latitude's about 55 degrees North," Yank announced, though with no air of finality. "We've got to keep her well off the coast a while. It sticks out to the west'ard plenty, just south of here."

"All County Mayo and Connemara's there," said Mike. "You're surely not going by all those lovely places now, Yank? I'd give my eye teeth to be going in there – any place there."

" 'Fraid it's all a bunch of rocks to us now, Mike. We've got to hurry past. If the wind came from the west now, we'd be in a fix. We're gambling, you know. The ship hasn't got large-scale charts for these little ports, either. She doesn't ordinarily come around here."

"There's big ports, too, Yank, my boy. There's Galway, on a bit, and there's Limerick south of that. Fine big cities they are, both." Mike looked aggrieved.

"Sorry, Mike. But we really daren't even go in close for a look until we can see the Fastnet, or Cape Clear. I promise you though, we'll do some coasting there, if the weather's clear. We'll go in so's we can hear the dogs barking on the farms. Not that we've got anyone who can recognise 'em, like Taffy can around Porth-Dinlleyn and Nevin."

"Indeed I can that," said Taffy, delighted to think of sundry hounds and other beasts he knew quite well by sight and sound, by Morfa Nevin. "And Mr. Hughes knows 'em all from Hell's Mouth right around to Barmouth.... Ah, Mr. Hughes, now. It's time he came to. I'll run down again and take a look."

Taffy was back in a few moments, with the report that Mr. Hughes looked much better than he had even an hour earlier. His eyes had opened, he said, when he went into the cabin. But he hadn't said anything.

"Maybe it's concussion he's got, as well as the nasty

cut on the head," said Taffy. "Maybe we ought to keep quiet and not disturb him."

"Old sailors don't get concussion!" put in Chum Jones.

"He must have something pretty bad to be out so long," Taffy argued. "Anyway I've been treating him for concussion, like it says in the 'Ship Master's Medical Guide' that's in the medicine chest."

"If he survived that crack on the skull he'll survive the treatment too. Boy, that man's skull must be iron!" said Chum Jones, with some envy.

"You're not very kind now to my treatment," said Taffy. "If you could speak the Welsh now, I'd be telling you something!"

"Peace, lads, peace! Is this what a spell of decent weather does to you? And didn't I hear somebody say something intelligent about keeping quiet a while? We'll start the holystoning up in the eyes of her if this is to be the racket. Come to think of it, that brass could do with a bit of a wipe. Who's watch on deck?"

The lads melted away rapidly. They had been grouped round the deckhouse, on the sunny side. All was quiet for a while when they had dispersed. The ship creaked gently along, her motion easy and her stride graceful, with perfect rhythm. Out here in the open North Atlantic the sea ran long and true, and there were no ugly holes in it as there were in Cardigan Bay and the Irish Sea. There was just life enough in the good wind to fleck the water here and there with a little white, to bring it to life. The ship was running a good seven knots, even with her reduced canvas, and she was steering like a witch. Her bows slipped easily through the long blue seas, and her wake astern was clean and straight.

So the day passed – the fourth since she had been blown out of Abersoch. Only four days! It seemed an age. All the lads now felt like resurrected shades of Columbus or Cabot or Cartier, or some one of the illustrious pioneers of the great sailing past. The tones of the B.B.C. announcer giving out what passed for news seemed to come from another world. Each bulletin now had some mention of the ship. The six o'clock evening announcer spoke lugubriously of some wreckage that had been found on the coast off Nevin, and of an aerial search that was planned in the Irish Sea. The wreckage was an old hatch encrusted with barnacles. How that could possibly have any connection with the ketch which had neither hatches nor barnacles, the news bulletin didn't say.

"Goats!" said Taffy scornfully. "Why don't they ever get a single thing right about ships! Hatches come off cargo ships. Barnacles take months to grow. As soon as any ship is alleged to be missing, some stupid ass is finding 'wreckage' from her! I bet that hatch was on the beach by Nevin when I was a boy."

"What are you now, Taffy?" asked Yank.

Taffy grinned.

"I'm hoping no poor airman will lose his life, looking for us where we aren't to be found," said Tiny, quietly. "That happens far too often."

"And still not a sign of a trawler to pass a report. It

must be very poor fishing around these parts, is it, Mike?"

"The best fishing in all the world!"

"Where's the trawlers, then?"

"Inshore, my boy. There's no need for 'em to come out this far nowadays. Why, half the crabbers out of the Bay o' Biscay come up here too, and the little purse seiners from Spain, taking fish by the ton. Its the best fishing in all the world."

"Sshh! You'll be waking the dead. . . . I'm worried about that B.B.C. report, though. Our people'll sure be getting bothered now. Keep a good lookout for fishing lights to-night, boys, and call me if you see any, any of you. We'll get a signal to them somehow."

The idea of unnecessary alarm was disconcerting. But what could be done? As Yank had said, they ought not to go much further without being reported by some kind of vessel. But the ketch continued to run, and there were no cargo vessels in sight making for Galway or Limerick, nor did they see a trawler. Big ships crossing the Atlantic made either for Malin or for Fastnet. The night brought no lights but the loom of some great lighthouses ashore, one after the other all night long, some nearer, some further, sometimes only the loom of the light below the horizon, at other times the light itself. Tiny timed the flashes and gauged the characteristics, to identify the bigger lights in the ship's Light List. She was heading due south, after midnight, more or less in line with the coast. As the hours passed without any sign of change of wind and the B.B.C. bulletins promised good weather, Yank allowed the ship to creep in nearer to the coast, intending to make the land boldly off the Blasket Islands or Valentia, in the morning.

Sure enough, the morning brought a blue haze of lovely land on the port bow. This was grand progress!

Hans, whose watch it was, had the wheel a little after dawn, with one of his watchmates aloft to see what he could make out of the land and the other in the galley brewing some brown wet stuff he called tea. The ketch was sailing beautifully and the morning gave promise of another good day.

Slowly Hans became aware that someone else was on deck. Someone else had come up the companion from the little alleyway below.

"Where's Moelfre now, boy?" a well-known voice roared from just for'ard of the mizzen. Its roar was weak, but it was still a roar. "Where's Moelfre?"

"Is gone, Sir," said Hans.

"Gone?" Mr. Hughes, reeling a little in the fresh morning air, looked absolutely bewildered. "Moelfre *gone?* What's happened then in Wales?"

"Ireland," said Hans, with an expressive wave of his hand towards the maze of the land.

Mr. Hughes gulped, staggered to the grating, sat down, and stared about him like a man slowly recovering from a bad dream. He put up his hand to scratch his head and found the bandages there, and looked even more bewildered. He stared to wind'ard and then to leeward, and stared at the deep blue sea, and he looked everywhere for the grey-green turbulence of Cardigan Bay.

"Moelfre gone? And Snowdon, Cader Idris, Moel Hebog, Bird Rock—all gone? *Ireland?* On *that* side of us?" he gasped. "Where *is* the ship?"

"Ireland," said Hans. "We go around."

"We go round? My head's going round," said Mr. Hughes. "What happened?"

"Storm," said Hans. "Gaff come down, Wham! Hit you. We cross the Causeway. You help."

"Crossed the Causeway?" Mr. Hughes looked like a man realising that what he'd thought was a bad dream had been no dream at all. Hans made his remarks, brief as they were, immensely more impressive by gesticulations and sundry sounds meant to represent storms, a flailing gaff, seas breaking on the Causeway, and maritime vicissitudes in general. Mr. Hughes looked at him, astonished. He kept peering in the compass bowl, at the land, aloft at the mizzen bent in place of the main, and out over the North Atlantic, in turn, as if he never would be able to make out what had happened. The arrival of the lad from the galley with a dish of powerful tea did something to revive him. The tea shocked him more fully back into consciousness.

"Tea, Mr. Hughes. It's grand to see you again on deck, Sir. Are you all right now?"

Mr. Hughes took the proferred mug. "Tea, you call it? You don't need a mug for this stuff, son, it'd stand up by itself! Ugh!" But the old Mate tossed it down with a grimace. "It'd start the engine.... How long have I been down below, lad?"

The boy reckoned up. "Maybe a week, I think, sir. But

I've lost a bit count of the days, like, since we started this voyage. I'll go call the Yank."

The boy disappeared and Yank was back with him like a flash, smiling to see Mr. Hughes on deck once more.

It took a long time to explain to the injured Mate just what had happened. When he understood at last—and this was not before the 8 o'clock B.B.C. news threw further enlightenment on the situation by more references to the Nevin wreckage and the air search that was to take place that day—he thoroughly approved all that had been done.

"You've done well, lads," he said. "Mr. Holt will be pleased. This is just the kind of voyage he'd like all the boys to get a chance at. But I can't believe it! You mean to tell me you have brought the ship right out of the Irish Sea and round most of Ireland, and that's County Kerry I'm looking at over yonder now, at the sou-west of Ireland?"

"Well, sir, it's where County Kerry *ought* to be. I'm not saying any more than that. But here's the plot, on the chart here. I was going to haul up a bit and get closer to the land, for identification, but I didn't want to take any chances on these rocks here. This Skellig, and these Bull rocks," pointing to them on the chart. "We've been lucky with the weather, once we decided to go round Ireland and not to fight the wind. But we can still get a dirty kick on to those rocks, I reckon."

"You're right, lad. Never trust the North Atlantic."

Mr. Hughes gave a close look at the chart, and carefully noted the way the ship had come. He sent for the deck book, and compared the patent log readings with the distances measured off, and checked the compass courses. Now and again he grimaced a little, as if his head hurt him. But he found nothing to cause him any pain in the record of that extraordinary run.

"And myself lying down below all the time," he kept saying to himself, as if he was trying to force himself to believe it. "And gales and fog and lee shores and a stream of ships and everything else. And now there are airplanes out looking for the ship, you say?"

"Yes, sir. That's what the radio tells us."

"We can't have that. We'll clap every stitch to her we can, and chase her along. Now, you get some lads to break out everything that's in the sail locker aft there. We'll find something to bend on the mizzen there, and maybe a rag of old stays'l that'll make a gaff tops'l to help that little sail upon the main, or something we can contrive for a spinnaker. The spinnaker itself is in the shed at Aberdovey. It isn't spinnaker time in Cardigan Bay, as you well know."

A gang of lads brought up everything that was in the sail locker, which was reached through a small hatch abaft the wheel. There were two spare jibs, an old stays'l, and a summer tops'l.

"Just as I thought," said Mr. Hughes. "We'll make do fine with this lot. Now, we'll bend this stays'l for a leg o'mutton on the mizzen mast. That'll balance her. We'll get the gaff tops'l set somehow, and we'll use yon other stays'l for a spinnaker while she can run."

Mr. Hughes was unable to get about. He sat on the

grating aft in the sun with his back against the carley float. Under his skilful and experienced old eyes the work of setting every possible stitch went on splendidly. He looked approvingly at the group of boys who were the crew. It was understandable that those with previous sea training would fit in and pick up the work quickly, like the two *Conway* boys, the Pangbourne lad, and Taffy from Nevin. He'd been born in a boat. So had the Icelander, like as not. And the Yankee lad had previous experience of ocean yacht-racing. But the others, why, they were working like veterans too – dark Pete, from South America, the lad who was an apprentice cook with the London caterers, the boy from Birmingham and the little chap from somewhere in the Cotswolds. And the young chap from Manchester, who'd looked so pale and pasty-faced when he came marching down to see the *Warspite*, alongside at Aberdovey, those few swift weeks ago. Now the whole lot of them acted and worked, and looked, like a real bunch of sailors – *sailing-ship* sailors. If he'd not seen something of the kind happen often before, Mr. Hughes never would have believed it. But the boys were all right! All boys were all right, given a chance, he mused. The miracle of the ketches happened every month at Aberdovey, though never before, quite like this.

Soon every possible stitch was set and drawing, and the ship bounded along. The wind freshened with the morning, and she had all that she could stand. She was running a nice nine or ten knots, and the coast of Ireland came up almost hand over hand.

The wind hauled out to the west'ard as the ship approached the corner. Bolus Head, Dursey, Sheep's Head, Mizzen Head raced by. The Fastnet came in clear view.

"I know that corner," said Yank, excitedly. "I know the way now!"

"So does the ship too, by the feel of her," said Tiny. "She's going like a scalded cat!"

Round the Fastnet she raced, close-to, and, with every stitch of canvas drawing handsomely, sheets taut and the spinnaker trying to lift her right out of the water, the big ketch romped along the coast of Southern Ireland with a great bone in her mouth, like a St. Bernard with a shank of ham, racing for its kennel.

"Go on, good ship!" said Mr. Hughes delightedly. "Fix me a bunk in the deckhouse, Yank," he added. "I'll spend the night in there. I've been time enough down below."

He looked at Yank a moment or two.

"It's a fine thing you did, you know," he said at last. "And you'd grand lads to help you. I'm all for a bit of sea room: this bit of deepwater sailing's doing my old bones good, split head an' all!"

M.D.C

13

The Rescue

THE good conditions continued through the night, for the wind seemed to swing round Ireland with the ship. For once, the forecasts were tolerably correct. The B.B.C. spoke of fresh to strong southerlies still blowing up St. George's Channel and in the Irish Sea, and promised at least another day of westerlies or west-south-west winds off Southern Ireland. The little ship ran on past Cape Clear and Galley Head and the Old Head of Kinsale, and the first light of day found her racing past the entrance to the Cove of Cork. Mr. Hughes was out at the crack of dawn, to see how she was faring and how the gear stood. He paused by the rail a moment, looking into the lovely Cork Harbour.

"Ah, Sir, couldn't we go in there, now?" from Mike. "It's the loveliest bay in all Ireland. It's a shame to be rushing past, like a bunch of Yankee tourists!"

Poor Mike was almost in tears.

"I wish we could, son," said the Mate. "But we have to use the wind while we can. It's fair wanting us to hurry back to Aberdovey. Now will you bend the flags I hand out to you, and we'll make our number and pass close by every lighthouse and lightship we see, so's we can be reported, and relieve the minds of them that's waiting ashore."

Mr. Hughes handed out four large square flags from the locker, and Mike secured them to the halliards on the main truck, and hoisted the flags aloft. They were coloured flags of the international code used by all ships, and the four together made the distinguishing signal of the training-ship *Warspite*. "MBVC," they said, which, to any seaman or coastguard with the appropriate book, meant at once "I am the *Warspite* of London."

"Somebody'll be sure to see that before long, and pass in a report of us," said Mr. Hughes, looking aloft where the four flags were straining at the halliards and blowing out bravely in the fresh morning wind. "Aye, and the sooner the better. Let's have some of that Iceland coffee, now!"

At the word coffee, Hans the Icelander came along the deck at the double, with a great grin.

"Mornin', Mister U," he said. "No Moelfre! By and by."

"Yes, by and by we'll be seeing Moelfre all right, if we go on like this," rejoined Mr. Hughes.

"I fetch the coffee." And down dived Hans through the companion without touching the teak steps, for already there was a grand aroma coming from the galley. Curly Mathieson was at work in there. The patent stove in the training-ship was the type which never goes out, if it is looked after at all, and keeps itself going with a minimum of fuel. It had two ovens and two large hotplates, so there was plenty of room to prepare a huge pot of coffee and all the breakfast the boys could eat, and bake a cake as well if you wanted to. There was plenty of hot water for washing-up. A little port gave light but no air, for the sea was frequently right over it. The galley deck was just big enough to provide working room for one and to allow another to squeeze in if necessary, and the whole galley was designed to be worked easily and efficiently.

Here Curly Mathieson was undisputed captain, and he knew what to do. He'd opened six large cans of Canadian sausages, a can of bacon to add flavour, and twelve cans of beans in rich tomato sauce, and had the whole lot in an enormous deep dish with a little fat which would soon convert the mess into a wonderful seafaring breakfast. There was no bread left, for the boys had been hard on that and it wouldn't keep for ever. But there were plenty of biscuits, and margarine, and marmalade, and jam, and there was still one can of condensed milk. The ship's motion was not bad enough to upset the cooking or the preparations for breakfast generally. Perhaps the boys were all thoroughly accustomed to it by that time. There were high raised edges, erected round both the narrow tables, to keep the dishes in place, and each boy's place had its own special fence rigged across the table to make sure his plate of food did not slosh about. It could jump off the board, of course—if he let it. But this he never did. The food disappeared into his throat much too fast.

Except for the three on deck, all the boys had breakfast together. It was a happy meal.

"It's only 150 miles to go from off Cork to Aberdovey

Bar, as I make it on the chart," said Yank, eating his seventh sausage.

"That's about it," said Tiny. "She was logging eight in my watch. So if she keeps that up, we oughtn't to be more than about twenty hours."

"Say twenty-four, allowing for a drop in the wind at night," put in Chum Jones.

"You'd better say thank the Lord if the conditions *do* keep up," said Mr. Hughes. "Let's hear what the B.B.C. has to say on the subject. It's just five minutes to eight."

"This is the B.B.C. Home Service," the announcer began, right on the dot. "Before..."

The boys let out a unanimous groan.

"...the weather forecast, there are gale warnings..."

Another loud groan.

"...in sea areas Iceland, Forties, Hebrides..." and many more areas, but not, thank heavens, the Irish Sea nor anywhere near the south of Ireland. There, the forecast was for south-west winds.

"It's always a gale off Iceland," said Tiny. "But where's this place Forties?"

"It's some miserable corner of the North Sea where the temperature never gets above forty," said Chum Jones.

"You mean Cardigan Bay, then."

"That isn't the North Sea!"

"It's nothing to do with the temperature, chaps," said Tich Edwards, with a great air of knowledge. "It's something to do with the latitude."

"Says who? No latitude forty goes any place near the North Sea! It goes through the blooming Mediterranean."

"My guess is it takes forty poor guys to guess the weather there," was Yank's opinion. "So it can't be near the Irish Sea. It takes only one guy to guess the weather in that place, from what I've seen of it."

"It's really a fishing area, I think," said Mr. Hughes when he could get a word in. "It's a forty-fathom bank in the North Sea."

The news had nothing further to say about the missing *Warspite*, for the moment. Mr. Hughes hoped the Irish coastguards would have had an opportunity to make out the flags, or the lighthouse man on Ballycotton, for they went in close enough for him to read the ship's name with a decent telescope. They had to keep further off Knockadoon and Helwick, for the course from off Cobh to Aberdovey was directly to the Tuskar light and on in a more-or-less straight line. They were disappointed when the one o'clock news declared that they were still missing, though it did speak of a "small sailing vessel with indistinguishable signals" which had been sighted off the south of Ireland. "Experts," the announcer continued, "were of the opinion that this was not the missing training-ship which they said could not be in these waters, and the description of the vessel does not agree with certain features of the well-known training-ship."

"Experts, my eye! I can just see those blooming experts, sitting in some comfortable swing-chair ashore," said Tiny.

"When I graduate," said Yank, "I'm going to be an expert. On any thing. You don't have to know a thing, so long as the other guys think you do. Preferably the guys who give you the job."

"Now don't go blaming the radio, lads," said Mr. Hughes. "The announcer's doing his best. It's the news he's supplied with he's reading. He doesn't make it, and he isn't an 'expert.' And as for the other 'guys' thinking you know your stuff, Yank, you'll find the world isn't fooled that easy."

By the time the six o'clock news came round, when the ketch was racing on past Carnsore Point with the Tuskar in sight, still going wonderfully after a glorious day, the radio had decided that the strange ketch with indistinguishable signals was probably a French fisherman, though by that time they had passed, and spoken, seventeen trawlers from Milford Haven, twenty-three fishermen out of Waterford, nine large oil-tankers some inward and some outward bound, two Harrison cargo-liners, a Clan liner, the Ellerman *City of Birmingham* (which they had gone near enough to see a couple of small elephants peering over the side, and to wave to the crew), Alfred Holt's *Hellenus* (which had clearly recognised them), the U. S. Line's *American Scientist*, the Hollander *Rijndam*, and the *Queen Elizabeth* in the distance, to say nothing of another score or so big vessels more or less hull-down on the horizon, and five large four-engined aircraft coming and going to Shannon airport.

"Well, blow me down!" said Mr. Hughes. "I don't know what we could do to advertise the *Warspite* better than we've done! Unless we could sail her into Portland Place there in London! I was hoping our folks would have their minds relieved this night. I was, indeed! The worry'll be spoiling the course, up at the school."

Mr. Hughes obviously put the course and the school even ahead of his own immediate relatives, if he had any. He looked forward greatly to a continuance of the good wind through the night, and to reaching Aberdovey in the morning.

"It's rum we don't see any of those airplanes that's supposed to be looking for us, Yank," said Chum Jones, as the boys were seated along the skylight, in the early evening. The gulls were shouting and soaring astern, now dipping down to pick up some morsel which Curly had flung overboard from the slopbucket, now giving a wonderful exhibition of perfect gliding, squawking the whole time.

"What's that?" suddenly shouted Tiny. "That's no seagull!"

He leapt to his feet, pointing into the sky. The boys followed his startled shout.

"There's one of your airplanes, Chum," said Curly, pausing at the rail with another bucket of slops. "And in trouble, by the look of her!"

"She's in trouble, right enough. Mr. Hughes!"

With the swiftness of a jet-propelled argonaut, a great four-engined machine came hurtling through the sky, steadily losing height, smoke pouring from both the starboard engines and the port outer engine brilliantly on fire.

With a great whish of air and a backdraught that made the big ketch stagger in her stride, the aircraft roared past, at a little over mast-top height. They caught a glimpse of a tense face through the cockpit glass, as the aircraft's captain fought at the controls.

"He's ditching!"

The big aircraft had turned into the wind, and was flying just above the sea, tail low. Now the tail struck the water which splashed up in a mighty cascade like the tremendous spout of some outsize whale or the base of a waterspout. Again the tail struck; again! The spray and spume covered the aircraft.

"He knows what he's doing! Good man! Taking the way off with the tail," shouted Yank.

"Stand by, everyone!" Mr. Hughes ordered.

There was an instant tense response.

"You go to the wheel, Iceland."

Hans jumped to it.

"Steer for the crash! Lads, now, stand by the spinnaker and get the gaff tops'l off her. Tiny, you and Edwards clear the boat. Get it off the chocks and swung outboard. Steady as she goes now, Iceland!"

The orders came with a bark and the lads leapt. The spinnaker came in as if the big ketch was a racing dinghy rounding a mark, and the gaff tops'l fluttered down in the twinkling of an eye. Boys leapt to give a hand at clearing the boat. Meanwhile the airplane had rocketted to a stop and it lay spread out upon the sea like a helpless piece of outsize tin, a big deflated can with its tail knocked off, and its enormous wings awash, as if it was putting out great arms to try to support itself. Already the water was lapping at the fuselage.

"She won't last five minutes!" said Mr. Hughes. "We'll run down. Stand by, lads, to lower the mains'l when I give the word!"

The airplane was now less than a cable away. The boys could see the American markings. It was a military machine, long and slim. They could see some men on one of the wings. A door was opened in the fuselage, and more men there were struggling with something that looked like a big sack. That would be their dinghy. The plane was settling steadily in the water. A figure in a yellow life-jacket jumped from the broken tail. They saw him strike out in the water, making for the wing.

"Stand by the halliards! Lower away! Boom 'midships, Yank!"

Down came the mainsail—or rather, the mizzen which was masquerading in its place—on the run, with a singing of blocks and a rattle of good cordage. They were near enough to shout now.

"Bring her up, Iceland! Steer for the port wingtip!"

Hans, imperturbable as ever, did as he was told upon the instant. The boat was ready at the falls.

"Hold the boat, lads!" Mr. Hughes shouted "I'm going to try to get those fellows off right along their wing. Ahoy there, airplane!" he bellowed, all inconvenience from his broken head completely forgotten. "Ahoy there! Get out on the port wing! Jump for't as I come by! Here, you shout to them, Yank. Maybe they don't get my accent."

"Hi, boys! On the left wingtip!" shouted Yank. "We'll sideswipe you and you jump!"

Several figures waved. The *Warspite*, even under her shortened sail, was rushing at the wreck of the airplane now, in the last of the daylight. The sun had gone down long before and there was a soft and lovely twilight. The scene was one of infinite peace, and promise of good-will. It seemed strange that men's lives should be at stake at such a time. But they would not be at stake long. Hans crouched over the wheel, Mr. Hughes beside him, saying nothing, watching the ship, gauging the distance, watching that big useless sinking thing and the jagged wing which could rip a fatal hole in the *Warspite*, if she misjudged, if she came too close.

"Watch her, son. You're doing fine," said Mr. Hughes. "Lads, keep clear from the starboard shoulder of her now!"

The jib-boom was in line with the jagged hole where the aircraft's tail had been. The sea was rushing into the broken fuselage there. Now the jibboom-end was by the wingtip.

"Down stays'l!"

Down the stays'l rushed.

"Down mizzen!"

Down came the little leg-of-mutton on the mizzen as if it had been set on an elastic string. The big ketch halted in her stride though still with manageable way. The aircraft rolled alee, raising its port wing out of the sea. At that precise instant, six figures leapt from the wingtip on to the *Warspite's* deck. Two of them landed perfectly. The other four landed on the first two. A seventh fell in the sea. Mike flung him a life-ring on a long line. He grabbed the buoy and they began to haul him in. Even as he was being hauled to the side of the ship, the mottled bulk of the huge aircraft slipped into the deep water, with a greasy gurgle like water running out of an enormous bath.

"Whew! Nice work, boys!" said a tall young man in the uniform of an American Army Air Force major, walking along the deck towards Mr. Hughes with outstretched hand. "Ossendovski's the name—Hiram L. Ossendovski. This is my co-pilot, Mr. Glass. Mr. Glass is from Dallas. And this is the navigator—a bum he turned out to be! Mr. Eisenblom. This here's Mr. Hughes. And Mr. Yamomoto, and Mr. Haleakala. Mr. Haleakala's from Hawaii. So's Mr. Yamomoto. We were on a training flight. Engine trouble," he added, laconically.

"Why its Owen Hughes from Criccieth!" shouted the American the major had introduced as Mr. Hughes. "Owen Hughes! Why, Owen!"

Mr. Hughes shouted something in Welsh.

"Blime," said Tiny. "He's found a long-lost brother!"

"It sure is a small world," said Yank.

The two Mr. Hugheses were jabbering away in Welsh together by the wheel as fast as they could go, all thoughts of recent rescues and imperilled lives and everything else forgotten, for the moment. But only for the moment.

"Put the sail back on her, my lads," Mr. Hughes remembered. "Give her back the lot. And resume the course for Aberdovey!"

"Aye, aye, sir!" sang the lads, and the rescued airmen gave a hand to set all sail. The ketch's bow was turned once more towards the Dovey bar, and she raced onwards.

14

Aberdovey at Last

"WHY dang it! There was a two-way radio in the dinghy," said the Major, when he suggested putting a message through to his headquarters.

"What dinghy, Major?" asked Tiny.

"Why, the one we ditched when you picked us up, son. That was a dinghy Johnny here was pitching through the escape hatch. Self-inflating, you know. They're wonderful things. Two-way radio in them, and all home comforts. Even an outboard motor in some of 'em, and a kite to fly an aerial so's you have a chance to send messages over a fair distance. Food, too. And yellow stuff to discolour the sea, first aid, and everything. Well, it's all gone now."

But the nine o'clock news, coming on in a few moments, dispelled all worry at any rate about the ship not having been seen. The *Helenus* report was given, and the whereabouts of the *Warspite* were once again known to the world. So they would be expected off the bar in the morning.

The American airmen settled aboard as if they were as much seafarers as airfarers. An animated group consisting of young Don Wiggins, Nick Senussian, Curly Mathieson, and Mike O'Leary listened open-mouthed while Johnny Haleakala regaled them with tales of old Hawaii, real and imaginary. None of the boys had ever seen a real Hawaiian before. Such figures belonged to romance. They stared at Johnny Haleakala—he pronounced his name something like Halee-akalah—as if they rather expected him to turn into a chanting Polynesian at any moment, and hoped he would. But it turned out that Johnny—or so he said—had been a cowboy on a pineapple plantation on the island of Lanai, before enlisting.

"A cowboy on a pineapple plantation!" said Don Wiggins, prepared to believe anything about Hawaii but unable to understand what a cowboy would do at a roundup of golden pineapples.

"Yeah!" said Johnny, delighted with his audience. "That's me, all right. That there pineapple ranch's so big, fellows, there's a cattle ranch to supply beef for the labour. I look after them steers. Why, that whole island is one big plantation. It's more'n a hunnerd square miles—bigger'n Wales."

"Bigger'n Wales my foot!" shouted Chum Jones who was near, unable to stomach that, though he never in his life had previously heard of Lanai. "It's about as big as Bardsey."

As big as Wales or not—and it certainly was not—it seemed that the plantation island of Lanai was a fascinating place, and the lads sat enthralled. It seemed that Lanai produced the most wonderful and the largest pineapples in the whole world, and the life of a cowboy there was one long horse-born holiday. Even George Yamamoto was listening intently. It turned out that Mr. Yamamoto in civil life was a waiter at a Filipino night club by Waikiki beach. According to him, so was Johnny.

Mr. Hughes' Welsh friend from Criccieth had emigrated to the U. S. A., after the war. He had been in the Royal Air Force in the '39–'45 mix-up. So he had enlisted in the U. S. Air Force after the fearful cold of a winter in Detroit had proved worse weather than anything even Tremadoc Bay had to offer. The two Mr. Hughes were jabbering away half the night. The Mate of the *Warspite* had been in the States too, many a time, as a sailing-ship sailor. The fact that his real acquaintance with it extended, in the main, to the case-oil berths at Hoboken shortly after the turn of the century, the Seamen's Church Institute on South Street, and the Bowery, did not in the least deter him from offering all kind of advice and recounting all sorts of reminiscences to his friend. It was a real sailor's yarn.

The major, who was a quiet man, was somewhat astonished, at first, to learn there was an American boy in the *Warspite*, and that he was at Eton.

"A student at Eton," he kept repeating over and over again. "Why, boy, whatever made you want to go there?"

"I didn't want," Yank hastened to explain. "It was my old man's idea. But it isn't so bad, sir."

As a matter of fact, he found himself remembering with rather a jolt that he actually did go to Eton, and what's more, ought to be back there the following week. It was going to be a bit of a shock, suddenly finding himself ashore again, and a school-boy.

At length Johnny Haleakala ran out of yarns, the major ran out of superlatives for the lines of the *Warspite* and the nice turn of seamanship the lads had shown picking up his crew, and the two Mr. Hughes had talked themselves out for the moment. The ship gradually settled down. The airmen were given bunks in the boys' quarters, on the settees in the comfortable saloon, and the major in the captain's cabin. The two Mr. Hughes stretched out in the deckhouse, to be handy for looking at the first glimpse of Wales in the morning, and soon all but the watch on deck were wrapped in slumber.

"Hearken for the Dovey bells!" they called to Yank. "And call us if you hear them."

Yank had the watch. He walked the small quarter-deck, balancing with perfect rhythm as the ketch rolled and ran along, as if he had been there all his life. He no longer noticed that the ship had motion. Was it only a week or so since they had come aboard? It seemed incredible. He looked up at the stars, watched the slow roll of the mastheads, admired the perfect grace of the wind-filled sails, went again and again for'ard in the eyes of her to listen to her tramping down the sea. Taffy was on lookout there. Taffy was silent, drinking in the peace and wonder of it all, too. The roll of foam before the bows was a pleasant sound and the wake stretched away phosphorescent upon the black surface of the water. Far off astern was the loom of the Tuskar light, and away on the port bow, the loom of another brilliant light which must be Bardsey. So far, so good! The west wind held and for once the skies overhead continued bright and clear. The wind had quietened somewhat, and the patent log showed that the ketch was running about six knots. It was a delight to feel the grip of the spokes of the wheel. Yank could not tear himself below when the time came for his relief.

"Better get some sleep," said Tiny. "Do you know what day it is?"

"Can't say I do, Tiny. I haven't been bothering much about the days. But let me see now, why, it must be Friday. Why?"

"And how long since we came to the school?"

Yank reckoned a moment.

"It'll be four weeks this Saturday—tomorrow."

"Well, my lad, it's tomorrow you'll be rushing round the mountains, you, and all of us. Last Saturday in the course, you know! That's mountain expedition day."

"Why, doggone. So it is."

Yank mused a moment.

"You know, Tiny," he said at last. "I sure hadn't thought of that. And if anybody'd told me just three short weeks ago that I'd be looking forward to running 35 miles around a bunch of North Welsh mountains any time between now and Kingdom come, I'd have said they were nuts, or worse! And yet now, why, I am!"

"Roll along, mountains! Good old Cader Idris," laughed Tiny. "But we will need some sleep, Yank. Or we'll find when we get ashore that we've got such good sea legs that our maintain-climbing legs are no good at all."

Yank grinned. But still he could not tear himself from the deck.

"Tiny," he said, "I'll tell you another thing that'll make you think I'm going nuts. I'm envious of you, you know, going to sea for life."

"Why not come too?"

"Can't. The old man has me booked for the U. S. Air Force."

"Well, it wouldn't be like this. I know that," Tiny went on, almost speaking to himself. "But it will have its moments. I'm looking forward to it—I always have. It's a man's life, serving ships. And an important life too. Somehow I just like ships—all ships. Why, if there's nothing else about, I can admire barges!"

"I'm envious. I am."

"You'll have your airplanes, though."

"They're noisy, tinny, and too darned fast! By the time I'm a pilot they'll all be jet-propelled and probably have retractable wings and turn into rockets soon's they're airborne, doing a couple of thousand miles an hour. They'll get everywhere so darned fast there'll be no point in going, or hurrying back, because soon's you're there you can be back again. I like the quietness of it here and—I don't know! The sort of feeling that it's *us* that's at least helping the old ship do her stuff. *We* matter here. You know, I've never felt so sort of settled in mind in all my life before, as I've felt on this passage here! Yeah, even with its worries, perhaps because of 'em. After all, we did lick them."

Tiny pondered over Yank's remarks.

"I've felt the same way too," he said at last, bending to the binnacle to get a rough bearing on Bardsey and the Tuskar loom. "I expect that's why they send us here."

"Rocket-driver – punk! Ah well, maybe they'll cost a million dollars apiece, and nobody'll trust me with one," Yank went on with some gloom. The soft light from the binnacle showed his young face puckered with worries. It looked so funny, so unlike Yank, that Tiny laughed.

"There'll always be ships to come back to, Yank," he said. "You know that chap who said 'I have had a lot of worries, most of which have never happened,' had something. You'd better start thinking some more about running round Cader Idris before you spoil your night's sleep – what's left of it – plaguing yourself about driving rocket-ships through the sky!"

" 'I have had a lot of worries, most of which have never happened.' You know, I like that. Good night, Tiny. Guess I'll go below. That Lanai cowboy's in my bunk, though."

"Use mine. Good night, Yank."

Yank tore himself away and loped off for'ard. Moments later, his tousled head was still to be seen silhouetted against the soft light of the night, looking out from the for'ard companion as he continued to muse upon the scene.

The Mate was called at his own orders at the crack of dawn, at the very first showing of grey in the eastern sky. There were no lights to make for at Aberdovey bar, and he wanted to check the landfall. All the lads were up before six, scrubbing the deck down, polishing brass, and generally getting everything spick-and-span and Bristol fashion for coming into port. The mackerel were abundant and a grand breakfast was assured.

A pale sun climbed slowly over the mountains and shone upon the bay, and as it dispersed the early morning mists the mountains themselves rose into view. Steadily the ship sailed towards them. Once again, all the wondrous backdrop of the grand Welsh scene showed in its loveliness. It seemed incredible that any gale had ever roared here, bringing these gentle waters to a violent tumult, making the whole coast a dangerous lee shore! Now, far off, even the peak of Snowdon smiled, and all the foothills vied to set the great mountain off, and the skyline was an artist's dream.

There were Cader Idris, Bird Rock in its wild valley, the tall mark upon the hill that showed the Sarn-y-Bwch patches, the big golfing hotel that was a good landmark by the entrance of the Dovey. The Dovey bluff showed fine and clear. Coming in from the south-west the pleasant little port showed open to the sea beyond the shelter of its bar. Now they could see the Outer Buoy, the refuge on the tidal flats, and the masts of the *Garibaldi*. Flags were flying from the staff at the wharf. Boats were coming out. Ah, here was Ellis Williams with his strong big ferry!

J.M.D.C.

The ketch had her best blue ensign at the peak and her Sunday house-flag at the main. Her brass-work gleamed and her teak decks were spotless. Even the brass letters of her name upon both bows were polished until they reflected the smiling sea.

The ferry was approaching rapidly and, with it, the big new launch from Swan-Hunter's Neptune yard and, back of them, all the fishing craft, the pleasure craft, and assorted vessels from the town. Dinghies and small craft that had never before ventured across the bar were dancing on the morning sea. All the dinghies, all the cutters, all the whalers, and the lifeboats belonging to the school were either under way on the broad estuary, or outside already. Another and another string of flags went up on the wharf. The *Garibaldi* was covered with them. The tall houses along the waterfront street were putting out flags. The sun shone upon all Aberdovey and the seaside town was looking its very best.

The fairway buoys came into view. The marks for making the bar passage were plainly to be seen. Yank went to the wheel, Taffy to the bows. Mr. Hughes stood by the wheel to con. Hans the Icelander had one lead line, Tiny another, standing in either bow. Now there was plenty of water on the bar! The breakers ran upon the bar with only a quiet sound, murmuring, as if they were promising ever after to be good. The sands of Borth were golden in the morning sun and the Dovey valley looked like the Bay of Naples.

The boat was alongside. Ferryman Williams, his weather-beaten face covered with a great grin, shouted a welcome. The warden of the school, Mr. McDermott, the first Lieutenant, smiling old Zim, and a host of distinguished gentlemen none of the boys had ever seen before leaped over the rail. These were the governors of the school and members of the Trust, who had hurried to Aberdovey in slow trains through the night, when they heard the good news that the *Warspite* was coming in.

"Well done, boys! Well done, Mr. Hughes!" a tall, elderly gentleman greeted them. "Are you all well? And all here? Ah, I see you've picked up some recruits on the way."

"American airmen, Sir, from a crashed plane.... We're all here, all right. But please do not congratulate me. I've had nothing to do with it all. It was the boys. They've sailed her right around all Ireland!"

"Why, bless my soul! You don't say! But what happened when you'd crossed the Causeway and showed the ship off the Bar here?"

"I was knocked out, Sir. Knocked clean out. It was the boys who looked after her. And they looked after me, too."

"Don't believe the Mate too literally, Sir," said Yank. "It was he brought us across the Causeway – he and Taffy here. That was the only time she was ever in a real jam. Without Mr. Hughes, none of us would be here, indeed! Us boys just took the line of least resistance, and ran off before the wind. It stayed south until we were out of the Irish Sea. So we *had* to come around Ireland."

"Well, well, well! This is the kind of passage I've dreamed about. But we mustn't arrange it too often now, must we, Mr. Hughes? Or Captain?" said the gentleman, turning to the *Warspite's* captain, who was looking very pleased to be back aboard.

Meanwhile the ketch was running through the approach channel towards the bar, Mr. Hughes watching the marks, the lads in the bows flailing with the hand-leads and calling the depths which were never less than three and a half fathoms, for it was nearly high tide. The ketch raced along when the tide got hold of her, as if she were a horse which had smelled her home stables. Now she was through the channel, across the bar, and all the estuary was as quiet and flat as a river-side meadow, except for the tide running swift and dark. Down came the sails, half-way along the short stretch between the bar and the wharf. Ferryman Williams came alongside to swing the ship head to tide and put her alongside, as gently as a new-laid egg, bows outwards to the sea. The wharf was black with people, many of whom had been brought by an enterprising coach proprietor from Machynlleth and from Towyn, and as far away as Dolgelley up the valley behind Barmouth.

"Hurrah for the Maintoppers!" shouted the lads in the cutters and the whalers. "Three cheers for good old Maintop!"

The youthful cheers resounded in the valley.

"Why," said the Major. "Was it you boys that brought the ship all around Ireland, without an officer at all?"

"It was that," said Mr. Hughes, "for I was unconscious

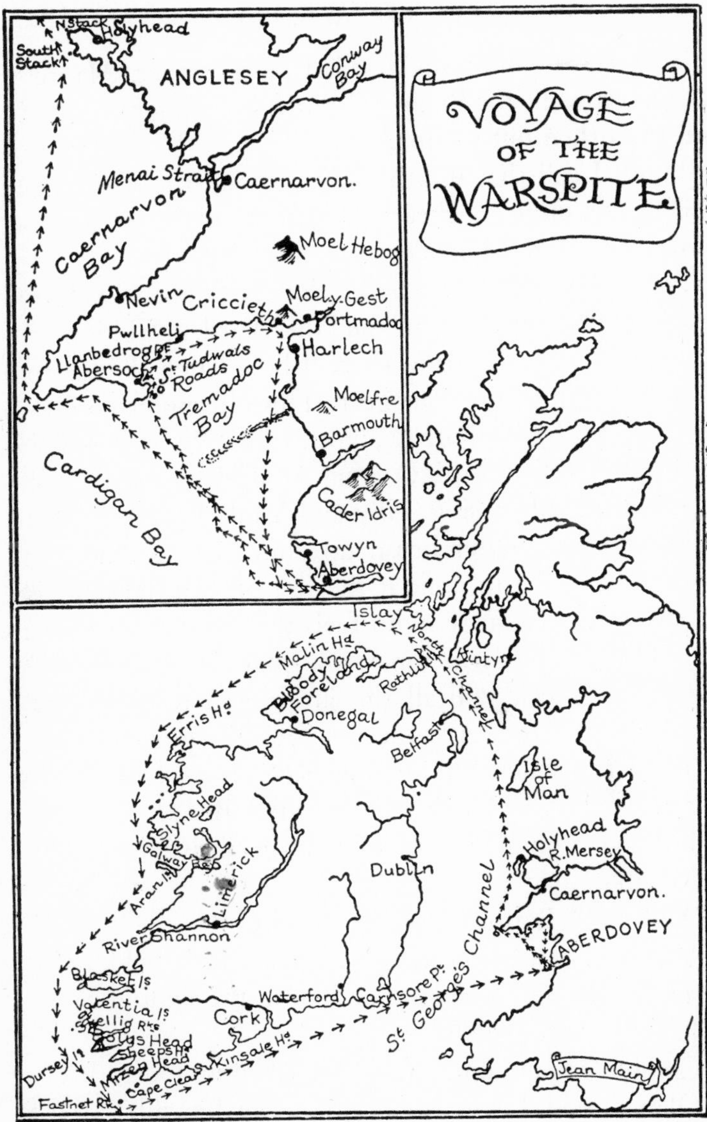
VOYAGE OF THE WARSPITE
N Stack
Holyhead
South Stack
ANGLESEY
Conway Bay
Menai Strait
Caernarvon.
Caernarvon Bay
Moel Hebog
Nevin
Criccieth
Moel-y-Gest
Portmadoc
Pwllheli
Llanbedrog Pt.
Abersoch
St. Tudwals Roads
Harlech
Tremadoc Bay
Moelfre
Barmouth
Cardigan Bay
Cader Idris
Towyn
Aberdovey
Islay
Malin Hd.
Bloody Foreland
Rathlin I.
North Channel
Kintyre
Donegal
Erris Hd.
Belfast
Isle of Man
Slyne Head
Galway Bay
Aran I.
Limerick
Holyhead
R. Mersey
Dublin
Caernarvon.
River Shannon
St. George's Channel
ABERDOVEY
Blasket Is.
Valentia Is.
Skellig Rks.
Waterford
Carnsore Pt.
Cork
Bolus Head
Sheeps Hd.
Mizen Head
Dursey Is.
Kinsale Hd.
Cape Clear
Fastnet Rk.
Jean Main

the whole way until she'd sailed past Fastnet. Maybe it was just as well, for likely I'd not have thought to do it! And it worked out so fine."

"Why, I call that worth a cheer," said the Major, and lined up his crew to cheer the lads from the wharf, too, before they hurried away.

"Now, Maintoppers, you've done extremely well and we are delighted to see you," said the Warden. "This morning, clear up the ship, and there'll be a truck down from the school to take up your gear. This afternoon you're to rest. Cader Idris tomorrow, you know! So rest up this afternoon. Briefing is this evening. Donaldson and Brown," he continued, addressing Tiny and Yank, "any spare time you have you'd better brush up your map-reading. And it would be no harm done if the rest of you did likewise. But any boy, of course, who feels that he doesn't care to face the mountain trip tomorrow may be excused. The doctor will check you all this afternoon. It looks like a fine day tomorrow. Anyone not feel like going?"

Complete silence fell on the eager boys for the first time since they had sighted the Outer Buoy.

"I'll have a go at it, sir," said Brum Shrivenham.

"Me too!"

"And me!" It was a regular chorus.

"What is?" asked the Icelander, slightly bewildered by the tumult of the welcome and now the announcement of the mountain expedition.

"Climbin' mountains," whispered Chum Jones.

"Okay," said Hans, obviously more bewildered than

ever. What *was* all this about mountains? An extraordinary lot, those English fellows: and when they found themselves mixed up with the Welsh in Wales, why! He gave it up, and slipped down below to boil some tea, for the coffee beans were exhausted.

"I reckon it's a good job we *are* going up the mountains tomorrow, Tiny," said Yank, up at the school late that afternoon. "This welcome's fair worn me out. And walking around these level streets is getting me down."

"You old moaner!"

Tiny laughed. And Yank grinned a broad, infectious grin.

15

A Silver Badge

"ANYBODY who spends a night on this mountain is bound to turn into a poet, or go nuts," Yank was saying to Tiny on the summit of Cader Idris. "I'm not hoping to spend the night here, but I feel *both* a poet and nuts, now! But just look at that view, and drink in this air!"

"All mountains do things to you," said Tiny. "But this—why, it really is something."

Below in all directions stretched the lovely panorama of North Wales. The day was perfect and had been so since early morning, when the boys first set off. To the west lay Cardigan Bay like a big blue plain. To the north, south, east, and every direction in between, lay the picturesque valleys with the peaks and spurs and hills rising from them, each fitting perfectly into the whole as if the panorama had been designed to be as beautiful and as breath-taking as it possibly could be. Little hill-farms nestled here and there. The big towns of Barmouth and Dolgelley (which Taffy called Dolgethly, or something like that) spread like pictured scenes against the hills and the sea. Behind Barmouth the tidal Mawddach showed no ripple to disturb its perfect surface. Below the southern

J.M.D.C.

slope lay the hamlet of Tal-y-Llyn, with its mountain lake and, to the west a little, Abergynolwen; down the Dysynni Valley was Bird Rock, looking curious from inshore and above it, when it had only been seen from the sea.

The whole glorious scene rolling away to giant Snowdon in the north and Nevin Peninsula looked as if it had spread itself out to be admired, and was basking in the mid-morning sun happy and pleasant. St. Tudwal's Roads, the harbour of Pwllheli, bluff Wylfa and Tryn Cilan, Bardsey in the distance, all showed up well.

"*Did* we ever struggle in a ship down there?" asked Chum Jones, puffing up. "It hardly seems believable."

Taffy was singing a song in Welsh. Brum Shrivenham was seated on a piece of rock, munching a fisherman's slice of bread and cheese, and staring amazed at the view, not saying anything. Mike, young Don Wiggins, Pete Cordoba, and Nicky Senussian were talking excitedly about the wild landscape all round them and mis-recognising everything. The Icelander was boiling a pot of tea in the lee of a lichen-covered clump of granite while he, too, munched at a great chunk of bread and mackerel with his free hand. Perhaps he was thinking of the briefing in Old Zim's cabin up at the school the previous evening.

"Don't you go and run off with our mountains as you did with the *Warspite!*" old Zim had said, grinning, "leaving our good Mr. Hughes to bring her back," he went on, dishing out flash-lamps, pocket compasses, rucksacks, first-aid kits, whistles, ordnance maps, instruction sheets, and advice, which was all to the point.

"Wear your strongest shoes, two pairs of woollen socks, and warm clothing, lads," he'd said. "Only eat when halted, and then slowly. And don't drink out of the mountain streams unless you've made sure the water is running, clear, and without any smell. And then don't drink much. And no calling at the tea-farms, either!"

Hans knew those tea-farms. They were famous places, dotted here and there on the hills where a boy could drop in for a really enormous meal, called tea. Tea was the least part of such repasts. Hans smacked his lips and decided that he wouldn't pass any tea-farms, if he could help it.

"Another thing," old Zim had said, "keep a check of your position whenever you can. You never know when a cloud might roll in, and you'll have to grope your way back. Keep a moderate pace. It isn't a race, you know. And keep together! That's the important thing. You're all divided into groups of six, each group with either the watch-captain or the vice-captain. Keep together, don't hurry, and don't dawdle. If there are footpaths, use them. And don't follow streams because water follows the steepest path, and you'll do better to keep to the shoulders of the hill that encloses the stream. When you're going up a mountain, use grass slopes if you can find them, and place your feet carefully so's not to dislodge stones and rocks. Somebody might be below. There'll be more than ninety boys scampering round Cader Idris, in sixteen parties. Remember your teammates."

Then Zim went over the routes in full detail, and made sure the boys thoroughly understood their maps and had mastered the pocket compass. It was all very thorough, very interesting, and very pleasant.

"One last thing," said Zim, "when you get back, report in. If you *don't* get back, 'phone. But everybody always has got back, so far, and you're the 8000th. And, remember this, you have to write an individual account of your expedition."

That was where Hans had become really worried.

"In English?" he'd asked.

"Well, preferably. But any language will do."

"Oh-ho!" said Hans, very dubiously.

He was still looking worried when he turned in, though he'd never been worried in the ketch.

Then, at the crack of dawn, off they'd all gone, the ninety-six of them in their sixteen groups, some one way, some another. Most did the first few miles by train. Some struck inland from Towyn and up past Dol-goch and Abergynolwyn to Tal-y-Ilyn, and up the southern slope. A few went to Machynlleth—Taff called that Ma-cough-hunllleth—but most of the others left the name unpronounced—and across country to the nor'ard from there, towards the mountain called Cader Idris. Others were to climb from Arthog. The routes were worked out to ensure that each party travelled something like the same distance in the day—between 35 and 40 good miles. Officers from the school went by bicycle and jeep to strategic points to check the parties and make sure all was going well. It was a well organised day, and everything went with a swing. Young Don tripped over a sheep on his first hill-side and the others roared at him. But that was the only accident, if you could call it an accident. Every one of those lads reached the summit of Cader Idris, as fresh as a young horse.

"I would never have believed it," said Tiny as they sat together over their sandwiches and Hans' 100-octane tea.

"Nobody ever does," said Zim, who was up there too. "I've watched their faces every time they first hear about this run, and they fall like an avalanche down the Matterhorn. But by the time the day comes, it's all a great lark. Sometimes there are storms, of course, and it's impossible to do a long expedition. Then they're all disappointed."

"You certainly feel good when you do do it," said Tiny.

"You know what I say, chaps!" began Chum Jones.

"It's a blooming, jolly, wizard good show!" they all shouted, before he could say another word.

"Yes, I'll stand by that," Chum Jones shouted defiantly.

"Well, lads, watch yourselves on the way down," was Zim's counsel. "Most accidents happen then. It's easier to turn your ankle going down than coming up. And ankles are rationed, remember—two apiece for life. Look after them!"

It was the very last of the lovely Welsh twilight when Tiny and Yank at last led their groups back to the school, after an experience that none of the boys was ever likely to forget. Then they fell at once upon a range of mountains of fish and fried potatoes stacked high on the mess tables, and demolished the lot in the twinkling of an eye.

Late at night, poor Hans was still puzzling over his essay on the expedition. He kept chewing a pencil until there was nothing left of it to chew. Then he'd borrow another and do the same with that. After an hour and a half, all he had in front of him was the same sheet of blank paper he'd begun on, and written on it was a heading only. "Expedition," it said.

"Hi, Iceland! Turn in!" Tiny shouted at last.

Hans grabbed the pencil with desperation, holding it as if it were an ice-pick. He stabbed it at the paper.

"Expedition," he wrote. "Bloomin' good show!"

Then he turned in.

The course was over, with the expedition. There remained only the tests—the five-mile walk and a mile run, and long and high jumping, and so forth. So long as a fellow did his best, he was all right. The tests weren't meant to produce a few champions for the others to sit and look at and brag about. The tests were contrived—like everything else had been—to bring out the unsuspected best in each fellow, and the standards were adjusted to age and individual ability.

The boys were set to beat their own previous best, and never mind about anybody else's.

"Cripes," said Nicky Senussian as he cleared four feet

eight inches, "I never jumped a blooming thing in my life before I came here, 'cept a queue!"

And he hurled the javelin 85 feet.

"I never had a chance to throw a javelin either," he explained, "so I'm going to chuck this one a good long way!"

He did.

The upshot of it all was that the Maintoppers came out at the head of all the watches. On the last morning, when the young sea-captain who was Warden of the school gave out the badges to those who had richly earned them, every boy in Maintop Watch found himself awarded the coveted silver badge! Nothing like it had ever happened in the history of the school. There was a special board in the entrance hall on which the names of all previous winners of the Silver Badge were inscribed, and it was a small board. The Silver Badge was not awarded easily. But now a new board had to be made, especially to take the names of the lads of Maintop Watch.

"Well done!" said the Warden.

Yank looked down at the silver badge shining in the lapel of his coat with a great pride, and so did they all.

The silver badges were still shining on the lapels of twelve assorted coats when the boys dispersed to go once more to the humdrum, ordinary world from which they had come, a few short weeks before. Most of them left from Aberdovey station, the same station where they had arrived. The *Conway* lads were travelling northwards through Barmouth and up to Afon Wen—so close to Abersoch—and ancient Caernarvon. Taffy went that way, too, though he was taking bus at Pwllheli for Nevin to spend a day or two at home before joining his ship again at Birkenhead.

The others joined the express at Dovey Junction which went up the valley to Shrewsbury, past Machynlleth and LLanbrynmaer and Caersws. At Shrewsbury they split up again, some for Liverpool and Manchester and points north, others for Birmingham, and Coventry, and Hereford, and Oxford, and London. Yank found himself wondering whether he would ever see them again.

The lads looked so odd, dressed again in their own clothes. But there was the stamp of the Outward Bound about them all—Don and Taffy, in their rough clothes and cloth caps, Chum Jones in the smart rig of a seagoing cadet, Hans with his blue jersey changed for a grey with an enormous roll-top collar and his flaxen hair imprisoned in a blue skull-cap. Brum Shrivenham sported an Hawaiian shirt in a gaudy floral pattern which he must have got from Johnny Haleakala. It was so bright it fairly warmed up the compartment and brought light even upon Shrewsbury railway station. Nicky Senussian's eyes were shining and the pasty colour had gone from his cheeks, and his spiv's drape coat hung oddly on his broadening shoulders.... Nicky was no spiv, and never had been. But he might have developed into one. The chances that he'd do so now were much reduced.

Yank sat back, as the express thundered along from Birmingham towards Paddington, and closed his eyes. Rough clothes, brass-buttoned reefers, fishermen's jerseys —long hair, tousled hair, broom-heads of crimson—dark skin, fair skin, red skin—from Iceland, Ecuador, Ireland, Wales, England, U. S. A.—what a lot of artificial barriers there were! And how they had all melted away in the clean sea air and among the rugged mountain-passes—the silly barriers, and all the flim-flam of life. Yank had heard a lot about the modern boy, much of which had been addressed to him. He'd thought it nonsense at the time. Now he knew it was. These lads were all right and they always would be all right, if they got the chance to feel they were alive.

That's what the *Warspite* and the hills had done for them. They'd felt they were alive—*really* living, not just getting up in the morning and putting clothes on, to shuffle through the day.

What was that slogan he'd read on the bulkhead in the ketch's saloon? Ah, he remembered it:

TO SERVE, TO STRIVE AND NOT TO YIELD

That was the thing. To serve the team—whatever team that might be—to do one's best, and never to give in. It was not a bad idea, at that....